Twist

Tales of Mystery & Mayhem

A Port Writers Crime Anthology

Foreword

I have been a member of Port Writers for many years. I have met a host of fine people, some great writers, poets and humorists. I have learnt and laughed a lot. It did therefore come as quite a shock, since reading this anthology, to learn that such a deep well of devilish cunning runs beneath the placid façade of those mid-north-coast locals with a literary bent.

In this work you will find historical murder mysteries, supernatural portents of disaster, red rose wielding rapists, buried loot, kidnap, forgery and other twisted tales.

I am certain that readers will find the stories as disturbing, engaging and enjoyable as I have. I also hope that it makes readers look twice at the familiar faces around them, the people you thought you knew so well, and wonder at the tortured soul that lies beneath.

John Byrnes is a successful mid-north-coast author of crime fiction. His debut novel 'Headland' was released in 2023 and achieved outstanding sales success. His follow up novel 'The Youngest Son' is scheduled for release in August 2024. John has been an attendee and member of Port Writers since 2014.

Introduction

This anthology was inspired by traditional mystery magazines such as *Ellery Queen Mystery Magazine* and *Alfred Hitchcock Mystery Magazine.*

It started with a competition for Port Writers Members to create a Crime and Mystery story of not more than 1500 words which had to have a crime of some sort that was central to the plot. This crime had to be a major part of the story – for without it there would be no story. From numerous entries the winner was *The Daisy Plains Gazette.* Other stories from the competition are in the anthology including the runner-up, *An Act of Treason Against the Crown.*

Later we ran a five-hundred-word challenge to write a story entitled *You Won't Get Away With It*, which had to contain something stolen and someone with a secret, as well as using the phrase 'you won't get away with it.' The best three stories, as chosen by Port Writers' members, are included in the anthology.

Rounding out the anthology are stories chosen from member's submissions of previously unpublished works. We hope you find each of these stories to be criminally entertaining reading.

Tom Penrose
Port Writers' President

Contents

An Act of Treason
Against the Crown

Susan Ash

Tom Bolton stood by the Thames in the gathering gloom of the winter's evening, watching the mist rise off the putrid, murky water and wondered how it had come to this. How all his dreams of success in the big metropolis had come down to a scrabble for money. Tom was a handsome man, tall and clean-shaven, with a hint of ginger in his side whiskers and thick chestnut hair. He looked like a gentleman in his new frock coat, but a closer inspection would reveal his breeches were worn and patched. Tonight, he had a harried look, furtive even, as if he were ashamed of what he might do. The sky held a pale milky moon, shrouded in wisps of fog. It cast a ghostly pall over the black slick of the river. He pulled his coat closer and shrugged his neck down into the high collar, feeling the moist air wetting his bare head. The toe of his boot caught the edge of the stone quay. Could he go through with this? He fingered the note in his pocket and felt the knife pressed against his calf in the knee-high boot. He tamped down all the thoughts swirling around his head. Thoughts of his wife, squandering their money on pretty clothes, and the beautiful Duchess who had invited him to her salon. He wanted to rise in society, to attend the salon and see more of the Duchess. To look the part, he needed a top hat to complement his outfit.

The hat in the window was a beautiful beaver skin. Nine shillings said the sign on its brim. He imagined himself entering the salon in that top hat. He could see the hatter inside in the glow of lamplight, who peered up at him thought the window. Suspiciously he thought, or was he imagining that? He straightened his collar, adjusted his coat, and stepped out of the damp night into the shop.

Robert Miller handed him the beaver skin hat. It sat tall and silky smooth on Tom's head. He looked this way and that in the glass, admiring it as he tipped the brim forward. He could feel the hatter's eyes on him so Tom began to feel uneasy. Perhaps the man could see the incongruity between the hat and his worn clothes. He dropped his gaze from the glass and straightened his shoulders. He fingered the one-pound note in his pocket again. Any further hesitation would make the hatter suspicious, so with a flourish, he removed the hat from his head, placed it on the counter and beside it, the one-pound note. Clearing his throat he said, 'I will take it.'

The hatter looked him in the eye for what seemed a long time. Tom dropped his gaze to the counter.

'Can you write your name and address on the back?' the hatter said finally, handing the note back.

He wrote George Clay, Eagle Street, all false. The hatter looked at him for a long time, turned the note over, peering at it. Tom could feel the sweat running down the inside of his armpits even though there was a chill in the shop. He looked nervously this way and that. Did the hatter suspect the note was false?

'Wait here while I investigate,' said the hatter.

'You have no right to detain me, I will go,' cried Tom.

He turned to leave but Robert Miller grabbed him around the back of his neck. A scuffle begun. Tom frantically tried to break free from the hatter's grip around his collar. Trapped and cornered, he struck out, hitting the hatter on the nose. Tom struggled out into the street where the cobblestones were grey and greasy, and he staggered.

'Stop thief!' the hatter hurled out into the darkness.

The next thing Tom was flung to the ground by the roving watchman. Robert Miller followed up soon after, mopping the blood from his face, his neckerchief all torn. Only then did Tom realise the enormity of the consequences. Tendering forged notes was an act of treason against the Crown.

He knew squalor but nothing like the cells of Clerkenwell Prison. The mist had come in from the river and the cold clung to the stone walls like a ghostly wraith. The smell of stale urine and rotting refuse hit him, and a wave of nausea surged up his gullet. His coat was no shield to the cold seeping up from the stone floor. He made out the other felons, clamped to the walls with chains from the rings around their ankles.

Tom knew tendering false notes attracted the death penalty and with a certainty rooted in his being knew he did not want to die. It was also difficult to tell the difference between a forged and a real note. There was so much public outcry when those caught tendering what they thought was a true note were caught and hanged. That could be his defence; he did not know the note was false. Nights turned into days and the creeping dread of his trial gnawed at his being. He was finally taken to the antechamber of the Old Bailey, where he shuffled forwards with the others on trial. The smell of fear wafted around the room, rancid sweat and the acrid odour of urine. The wooden planks of the floor were worn down by countless prisoners chained at the ankles, shuffling through. He could feel the sneers of the men surrounding him, but he held his burnished head up with a semblance of pride. One man sang out 'He's for the drop!' following the latest one to be called before the judge and jury. Tom considered this for a moment. Would he receive that dreadful fate? Hear the terminal words. 'Guilty. Death by hanging.' He imagined himself swinging from a gibbet, his tongue protruding till his neck broke, the final reckoning staining his breeches. He tried to force the panic rising in his gullet down into his stomach.

The door swung open. He was pushed forward by the guard so roughly he almost stumbled into the main courtroom and was momentarily blinded by the light shafting through the dirty windows high up above the bench. They were streaked with dirt and bird shit, chirruping swallows flitting around inside. A smell of mould hit his nostrils, damp patches showing on the walls and ceiling. Tom stood surrounded by a corral of polished wood, the prisoner's dock. He gripped the rail to steady himself and felt the smooth, dark wood in his palms. It was slightly comforting. To his left and slightly below him sat the twelve jurors, arranged in rows of four. Across the room bathed in the light from the windows sat the prosecutor, already nodding to some of the gentlemen in the jury. The courtroom was a sea of black, grey, brown and beige with the occasional splash of white bodice and bonnet. Everything had a worn and dirty sheen. Tom faced the seated rabble desperately seeking out a familiar face. There was a rumble of feet scraping the floor as the bailiff called out,

'All rise!'

A hush descended as everyone looked to the raised balcony where the judge appeared in his crumpled black robe and yellowing wig. The trial began. The bailiff read out his name and the prosecutor started to read the evidence. 'On the seventeenth of November, Tom Bolton went to Robert Miller's shop to tender a one-pound note.'

The evidence continued until finally the watchman was called. 'We took a knife off him at the watch house. The prisoner was very agitated.'

Tom remembered his desperation in the watchhouse. The watchman had asked about the note. Where had he got it and who else was involved. Realising he was likely to bring all his connections into trouble he had stated, 'It is nothing! I will not tell you and bring four or five people into it.'

At least he had not betrayed his wife and her friends. He was not a snitch. Tom knew even if he claimed he did not know about the note being forged, the fact that he had struck Robert Miller and carried a knife was not going to save him. He watched the judge, who raised his yellow head and focused his rheumy eyes on Tom. He fixed his eyes on the judge's prominent red nose.

'So, you think your dandy clothes are going to save you, eh?'

Tom nodded weakly. The judge's huge signet ring flashed in a shaft of sunlight, as he raised the heavy wooden gavel to pass judgement. The sound of rustling and hushed whispering floated around the room with a hum of expectation.

'Guilty!' came the verdict.

Tom's heart sank.

Then, 'Fourteen years transportation!'

The relief washed over him. His knees felt weak as he clung to the polished rail.

He was not going to hang.

An Atrocity

Robin Mearns

Was it a crime or public mischief? Please be the judge. Allow me to give you the background information and then details of this true occurrence. It involves a devoted couple by the name of Simpson - husband John and wife Elizabeth who were the victims in this story.

When World War II broke out John enlisted in the RAAF. Initially, Elizabeth and their two little girls (a baby and a two-year-old) moved close to each area in Australia where John was receiving training. They spent as much time as possible with him.

Following his departure overseas Elizabeth moved to Sydney and rented a flat in a block of six. Now without John, she was determined to create a happy and stable life for her children, even though it was wartime. She was a wonderful mother and gave her girls her absolute love and devotion.

Elizabeth kept busy sewing and making all their clothes and becoming involved in charities and school committee work. She always sang as she went about the housework. There was never a hint she was worried for John's safety while he served in New Guinea and Borneo.

The girls enjoyed birthday parties, dances, and many picnics and games with their mother's close friends and their children. Special parcels from John were cherished.

John's letters were heavily censored. He only briefly spoke of life in the RAAF. He tended to concentrate more on his comradeship with fellow servicemen. He sent photographs of their life - including washing day in the bush.

In Elizabeth's letters to John she told him of daily events at home and sent photographs she knew he would treasure. They discussed their life's dream - to open a jewellery shop. They made plans for its implementation which gave them a vision and hope for the future

Eventually wonderful and almost unbelievable news:

The war was over!

Overwhelming relief and excitement spread throughout the world. Brightly coloured neon lights once again lit the night skies in contrast to a wartime blackout.

Details of the ship bringing John home were received. Soon they would have the joy of being together.

They were filled with anticipation and happiness as they set out to bring him home. It was a perfect Sydney day of blue skies and sunshine.

Elizabeth had written John's name in large letters on a sheet which they would display to help him find them in the waiting crowd on the wharf.

Families waited patiently until the swarms of servicemen disembarked. Then there were jumbles of happy, smiling people hugging and kissing. Laughter filled the air.

But they couldn't see John.

Was he on another ship and arriving at a different time and place? After all their joyful anticipation there was now only deep disappointment. What had happened? Where was he?

Buses began taking men to process their release from service. There was no sign of John.

They returned home with heavy hearts.

The girls were sent outside to play and shortly afterwards were called in for lunch.

They tried to enter the flat but the door wouldn't open fully. Then …

John popped out from behind the door!

There were squeals of joy as they kissed and hugged.

What a magnificent surprise!

He would be staying with them now: no more long separations.

In 1948 John and Elizabeth achieved their aspiration and opened their jewellery shop.

Elizabeth took delight in ordering jewellery, crockery, cutlery, and ornaments. John chose the watches and clocks. They enjoyed working together and their contact with many customers. Arranging displays of their carefully chosen stock brought satisfaction and pride in their achievement. Life was good.

They agreed the result of careful saving and planning over many years was definitely worthwhile.

John further enhanced his skill in repairing watches with movements, and recreating parts that were no longer available for grandfather and grandmother clocks. His reputation and expertise became widely known. He offered the service of travelling to the location of the clock and restoring it on-site. That service offer would lead to atrocious mental cruelty.

Elizabeth was a country girl and even with her busy lifestyle retained the habit of caring for and helping neighbours.

Their closest neighbour was Miss Campbell, an elderly Scots lady living on her own. She was on a pension and, she told Elizabeth, struggling to survive.

To supplement her income Miss Campbell sub-let part of her flat to a married couple. They, and she, had their own bedroom and sitting area but needed to share the single bathroom and kitchen. Initially, it worked well despite close contact. As weeks passed the couple became more and more verbally abusive to their landlady. She became a bundle of nerves.

Miss Campbell was in tears as she outlined the situation to Elizabeth and was close to breaking point. She couldn't stop shaking. Her life had become a complete misery, she said. She had asked her tenants to move but they refused and after each request increased their abusive behaviour.

Elizabeth offered to accompany Miss Campbell to the Chamber Magistrate at the local courthouse to establish what could be done. He advised a course of action to Miss Campbell.

Knowing her neighbour's fragile state of mind and health, Elizabeth supported her by accompanying her to subsequent meetings with the Chamber Magistrate and then discussing the outcome with her neighbour over cups of tea.

A court order forced the tenants to move out.

They severely damaged her flat before leaving.

Some weeks later the telephone in the shop rang. John answered and was told by the caller they wanted him to come and attend to a grandfather clock, a family heirloom, which was very precious to them. Unfortunately, it was nearly an hour's drive to the address he was given. Because of his interest in ancient clocks, he said he would leave shortly. Elizabeth was happy for him to go though it meant she would be left in the shop without assistance. He packed items he might need and cheerfully drove off.

Within half an hour of him leaving, the shop telephone rang once again. A woman told Elizabeth it was a city hospital calling. She said John had been involved in a serious accident and was admitted to the hospital with severe injuries which could lead to death. She told Elizabeth to get there urgently and gave her a number to ring to check for further details of his condition and his location in the hospital and rang off quickly.

When Elizabeth tried to ring the number, she was given it was not connected.

Telephones of the day did not provide for tracing calls. She was now unable to contact the hospital again.

She did not know the name or location of the hospital.

What could she do? She was alone in the shop.

She began desperately ringing every hospital in the Sydney area giving John's name and description and the scant information she had regarding the 'accident.' Each call drew a blank. No hospital she contacted knew of John or his injuries. She didn't know where to turn.

After almost an hour she was no closer to finding him. The anguish, panic, and desperation of getting nowhere clouded her brain. The dread of him passing away was unimaginable. He was her rock.

Elizabeth was at a screaming point - not knowing what to do for the best. Tears wouldn't help. She had to keep her wits about her and take the best action to find him. She decided to shut the shop door so she would not be interrupted. This was not the time to be dealing with customers.

She walked to the door. Her hand was on the lock. Now tears were streaming down her face, her hands were shaking uncontrollably and then - in walked John!

That's when she lost it and collapsed into his arms. He held her tightly as she poured out the horror of her experiences.

He told her when he arrived at the given address it was a vacant block of land.

He knocked on doors in the neighbourhood and enquired about the people who wanted his assistance. It was a waste of time. He didn't have their telephone number or any details about them and so returned to the shop.

It took many weeks and sleepless nights to get over the shock of what had happened. What a terrible occurrence - one difficult to forget.

They couldn't believe anyone could conceive such a cruel and heinous plan.

What type of people would be responsible for deliberately causing such extreme mental anguish?

Why?

Some months later Elizabeth bumped into one of Miss Campbell's ex-tenants. She had a smirk on her face. She said they had heard of the Simpson's recent 'troubles.'

It became quite obvious by her snide remarks who the villains were in the incident.

But what could be done about it?

There were only telephone contacts.

No hard evidence.

So, what is your verdict?

Crime for the anguish caused, or public mischief.

Buried

Wendy Haynes

Josie's mother Ellen was like clockwork. She peeled herself from the well-worn sofa when the taxi driver honked the horn. Every Friday night she was gone for at least an hour, some weeks longer if she had some luck on the pokies – what a waste of money. On her return, Josie's mother would spend the rest of the weekend in a drunken stupor after her usual trip to the bottle shop. A cheap drunk sucking down up to five casks of white wine over the entire weekend.

'Bye, love. See you in about an hour,' said Ellen as she grabbed her handbag and pushed the fly screen door open.

'Bye, mum.' Josie went straight to her room and waited.

Nigel, AKA, Fat Albert as Josie called him, was her mother's booty call. She'd met him at the pub a few years back. As far as Josie worked out, her mother was the cake and Josie was the icing. Not now. Never again. I hate cake!

It wasn't five minutes before she heard Nigel clamber through the back door. His last move, so it turned out. Josie was ready. Her breathing quickened, her heart pulsed hard and fast, and her thin body shook. Josie got a sense of when it was coming – the sick fucker never missed a beat. But this time, the beat played Josie's tune.

She'd set this plan in motion a week ago when she had found the heavily wooded spot about five hundred metres from a well-used bush track when she managed to escape the grip of her tormentor. The attacks were more frequent and brazen – to the point that her mother would be home in a drunken stupor and never once noticed Fat Albert drag Josie into the bedroom. It had to stop! No sixteen-year-old should have to take matters into her own hands.

On a mission, she had caught the bus into town yesterday afternoon. She plucked a big ass lock of the shelf from the Reject Shop and buried it deep into her backpack. She was in and out without a fuss. That night when her mum was asleep, she secured the lock to her door the best she could.

She heard Fat Albert pound up the short carpet-worn hallway, turning the knob of her bedroom door. When he realised it was locked, he bashed the door with his fat fist.

'You know you want it Jos. Come on, be a good girl for Daddy.'

'You sick fuck. You're not my father, you piece of shit.'

He was silent for a minute. Josie dragged the shovel from under her bed and positioned herself next to the door, ready to swing. Then he yelled again, 'Open the fucking door now you little bitch.'

Josie could hear the irritation in his voice. He was pissed. She knew he wouldn't stop until his urge to conquer had ended.

'JOSIE. Open the door or I'm going to break the bloody thing down.'

He was getting irate now. His voice boomed through the cracks of the door invading her room. That's gonna stop soon.

'You can't get me now. You, big lump of lard,' she teased. Josie heard Fat Albert snorting with anger and readied herself. With one short run-up and the weight behind him, Fat Albert bounded through Josie's room, pushing the paper-thin door flat to the floor. As he entered, Josie swung the shovel straight into his fat blubbery gut. He buckled over like a rag doll, and then Josie swung again and drove the shovel up to smash him in the face. He fell flat on his back, unconscious.

Josie looked down at the man who repulsed her, made her skin crawl, and gave her nightmares. She grabbed a half-damp towel from the rail in the bathroom opposite. She wrapped it tight around his face and head, raised the shovel, and started pulverising his face. Blood and gross stuff oozed through the once light pink towel. Josie beat the life out of Fat Albert like he had beaten the life out of her.

She raced out to the junk-filled yard and dragged the sliding trolley into the hallway. Fat Albert used it to squeeze his fat body under neighbours' cars to fix them, all cash jobs. She had to be quick in moving the body. Her mum would be back within the hour. She heaved his limp body onto the slide-trolley hauling it down the hallway, through the kitchen, and out the back door.

The grass was knee-high, the clothesline tilted, bent, and rusted. Her dog Ox a small Fox Terrier started barking.

'Shh. Ox, shh. Quiet boy.' She looked about, hoping none of the neighbours would stick their heads over the fence. They should all be sitting cosy in their homes.

Fat Albert was a creature of habit. Particularly when he was working on cars. She reached into the old Camira, light blue, auto, and buried her hand under the mat on the floor of the driver's side. Yep, she dragged out a set of keys and sunk them into the ignition. It took several attempts to manoeuvre the bludgeoned body onto the floor in the back of the car.

Josie raced back into the house to cover her track, mopping up any suggestions of blood. She grabbed another towel out of the hallway cupboard. She was worried about the door. Her mum would notice that. But she'll figure something out.

Returning to the car she covered Fat Albert's body with the towel, almost vomiting at the sight of the blood and meat-soaked towelling. Josie threw the sliding trolley on top of him and jumped into the driver's seat. She took off down the road trying her best to stay on the correct side of the road, she had only had four driving lessons so far, and it was dark.

Josie parked the car slightly off the road close to the opening of the track. She turned off the engine, cut the lights, and opened the door. She walked around to the passenger side looked around, listened, and waited a few minutes before opening the back door. The cold slight wind pressed on her sweaty hairy arms. She shivered. She dragged her mobile out of the back pocket of her jeans, now smeared with blood. Seven-thirty it read. Murder didn't take long; it's covering your track that takes time.

First, she planted the sliding trolley on the nature strip and dragged the body from the car onto the platform. She tugged it as far as needed, hidden in the scrub in case another car drove past. She then went back to the car and carefully wiped down every surface she had touched. She knew the cops were bound to come around. But she could just say she had had a few driving lessons with Nigel, and that would be the end of it.

Once she was satisfied with her clean-up job on the car, Josie scrambled back to the body and dragged it deeper into the woods.

Vodka freezes you know, just like a heart can be frozen and be incapable of love. She wondered if hers would ever thaw after this and all she had been through. She also wondered if killing Fat Albert had done any favours for another girl like her. How many lives had he penetrated?

The wide and mostly dug-out shallow hole between dead woods and flourishing underground was well hidden. Josie hoped it would be a long time until Fat Alert was found, if ever. As she dug the remaining soil from the hole, she swore she would never find herself in a situation like this again. Ever!

It took several hours before the hole was deep enough. Josie's hands were raw and sore, a mixture of blistered weeping skin, stained with blood. She stood half-bent, leaning on a shovel sucking in the air but it wasn't coming quick enough. She briefly closed her eyes, weary. She checked her phone, 11.31 pm. The bushland that surrounded the quiet suburb of Innes Lake was the perfect departure spot for Fat Albert.

His lifeless body lay beside the shallow grave, just deep enough for his bulging mass, it would have to do. His face smashed in, almost unrecognisable. Brute strength and cunning fed by adrenaline, and the need to escape gave Josie the chance to finally rid her of this paedophile.

She threw the shovel aside and pushed the corpse with her feet getting a weird sense of pleasure. Kicking at it as it rolled and thumped across the dry dirt and eventually landed in the hole. That's the end of you!

She shoved and pushed Fat Albert deeper into the hole with her feet, stamping, jumping, and walking over his body. Grabbing the shovel, Josie piled dirt over him until he was entirely covered. She then used the back of the shovel to pat the earth down hard.

Wiping the handle of the shovel with her t-shirt, she threw it like a spear as far as she could into the bush. When she got back to the street, leaving the car there, she dragged the car keys from her front pocket, wiped them carefully, and threw them down a drain as she walked home.

She walked in the door it was 12:45 am. Sneaking through the back door, she scooped Ox up on her way through and placed him gently on her bed. She could hear her mum snoring and knew it was safe to make a little noise. Firstly, she showered fully clothed and then stripped scrubbing her skin hard making sure she scrubbed under her nails. She then chucked her clothes including her shoes into the washing machine and added a double dose of detergent. While she waited for the washing machine to finish its cycle, she found a screwdriver, reattached her door to the hinges, and removed the lock. After hanging her clothes to dry she fell into bed.

She slept until noon Saturday and found her mother on the thread-bare sofa in the lounge room watching some crap on television about penguins.

'Hi, mum.'

'Hi, love. Sleep well?

'Yes, like a baby.'

Her mum turned and looked up at her through the haze of cigarette smoke. 'I could have sworn you weren't here, and your bedroom door was busted.'

'No, I was here. You said goodnight to me at about 10 pm. Can't you remember? And you can see there's nothing wrong with my door.' Her mum had blackouts all the time. Josie was often out visiting friends or walking the streets; her mother none the wiser.

'Oh.' Ellen frowned. 'And have you seen Nigel? His phone's here.'

Shit. 'No, that's strange. He must have left it here last week.'

'Umm. Must have,' her mum agreed with a frown.

The next day Josie grabbed Fat Albert's phone handling it with a tissue and pocketed it. She then walked to the end of The Point Drive and threw it in a bin sitting on the curb waiting for collection. She anticipated her mother's question. 'Where's Nigel's phone?' To which she would reply, 'Oh, he came over while you were asleep. He didn't want to disturb you.'

Josie spent the next few weeks attending school, hanging out with friends, and enjoying life as a somewhat normal teenager. With Fat Albert out of the way, she felt free and open to a better outlook, a new path forward. But there was always the lingering feeling of uncertainty. Will the police find the body? And will they uncover the truth?

During that time her mother Ellen had called over to Nigel's place several times, but he was never there. In the end, her mum gave up. Also, during that time, Robbie, the owner of the blue Camira came around demanding his car back, but Ellen and Josie just sent him on his way 'Talk to Nigel,' said her mother. It seemed no one missed Fat Albert.

But a month later Josie and her mum were parked in front of the television shovelling down 2-minute noodles while watching the 6 o'clock local news. It was announced that the body of a man in his forties was found in bushland in the quiet suburb of Lake Innes

'Oh, my God, that's just down from us. Look, Josie.'

'Shh, I want to hear it, mum.'

The news presenter said, 'Police inquiries have led them to Robbie Dean, known to police for previous convictions of assault and domestic violence. He has been charged with the murder of Nigel Banks, and other offences.'

'That bloody mongrel,' said Ellen.

Josie, sprung from her seat, elated. Two for one, perfect. The cops won't be coming here. She never liked Robbie much.

'What are you so excited about,' her mum said, watching Josie do a little dance.

'Oh, nothing. Just practicing my moves for our school gala dance in a few weeks.'

Cat and Mouse

Melanie Wass

Driving home from a mediocre day at the office was a predictable event for Laura. She had been making the same trip day-in, day-out, for seven years. Even though there were occasional variations she was a creature of habit and took the same route nearly every day. Falling into automatic pilot mode meant she could process the events of the day while still getting home safely.

Today, she was processing the unexpected news that a friend, Margo, had been diagnosed with an inoperable tumour.

"Yeah, it sucks big time," said Bethany after telling Laura. "Just shows, you gotta grab what life puts in front of you: never know what's around the corner."

Laura drifted along, homeward bound, as usual. With around thirty-five minutes of driving time still ahead of her, recognition hit. Almost simultaneously, both her subconscious and conscious minds fused to focus on another vehicle that had been darting in and out of traffic around her. Each time Laura passed it, the car came from behind and overtook her amidst the traffic.

At first, Laura was no more aware of this car than any other on the road; simply another part of the traffic to be negotiated. When you travel the same route every day, at the same time, you get to know other cars which are regulars. But this car was not one of them. At some point in the past few minutes, coincidence became a pattern rather than a segment of random traffic flow. If she changed lanes, the other car would follow. At times, there would be several cars between them; most times they were head to tail, sharing the lead. Occasionally Laura would lose the other car, then it would suddenly loom up from behind or she'd see it slowly moving up front, as if waiting for her to catch up.

Initially, Laura was annoyed. Then a little scared. Finally, she was challenged. Laura was being drawn into a game: cat and mouse.

The Car was a shiny Alfa Coupe: a few years old but obviously well-loved and well-cared for. Crisp white with sleek muscly lines, the legendary badge sitting tauntingly front and back. Its windows tinted black so no matter how hard she looked, Laura couldn't see in. Trailing behind, Laura caught herself admiring the deftness of The Drivers' ability. Darting adroitly amongst the traffic; recognising trouble spots; evading blockages; driving on the edge of recklessness. Laura began to synchronise with The Car to the point where they became a team. It was almost as though they were on a racetrack with obstacles; a pair of precision drivers in superior machines demonstrating their expertise. Laura found herself smiling, settling into a more comfortable, more controlled position, with the radio louder and yet in full concentration - in tune with The Driver.

Eighteen minutes into the pattern, coming over the rise, Laura lost sight of The Car. She knew it was ahead of her only by a few hundred metres and yet, there was nothing. Clear space all up and down the roadway. A surprising sense of loss ran through Laura. She scanned ahead and behind again - no sign of it. Deflated, Laura pulled over to the kerb.

Taking a deep breath to settle her adrenaline, Laura sunk back in her seat and closed her eyes to rest. Admonishing herself for being so childish and irresponsible, she also had to chuckle silently - she'd got a huge kick out of it. She enjoyed matching her driving skill; meeting the challenge thrown down to her. It gave her a taste of her dream - to just once do a circuit around the Mt Panorama racetrack at Bathurst.

Opening her eyes, Laura realised the territory was unfamiliar to her. She'd been led off course in the heat of the game. To get her bearings she started looking ahead and to the side for landmarks. Houses. And more houses. Not a thing familiar. Glancing in her rear-view mirror, Laura caught her breath: it was there! The crisp white Alfa was throbbing quietly just behind her. Laura's pulse began to rise rapidly. Startled, she waited with her eyes fixed on the sight in the rear-view. The tinted windows of The Car still gave nothing away. She heard the engine being cut and impulsively reached for the door handle. Trepidation and anticipation mingled with a fear of embarrassment as she lifted herself out of her Mazda MX-5 and began walking toward the vehicle behind. The sound of her footsteps pounded in her ears.

She approached The Car, and its mysterious driver. A sense of excitement overwhelmed her as she heard the windows electronically open.

"Well, congratulations. You're an extremely competent driver - I must compliment you."

Laura was taken aback by the words - no, more by the manner in which they were delivered. Like honey. Like a Svengali spreading honey. She was intrigued and beguiled to the point of feeling very light.

"I have to confess," she stammered falteringly, "I enjoyed it."

"I know." smiled The Driver. "You look a little flushed - perhaps we could enjoy a drink?"

"Where would you like to go?" asked Laura.

"How about here?"

"Here?" Laura asked incredulously glancing about the residential street as she tried to spy a bar, hotel or bistro she obviously had not spotted.

"Yes" came the silken reply, enjoying Laura's confusion. "This is where I live" said The Driver pointing to the rambling cottage they were parked alongside.

They were still playing cat and mouse, realised Laura. All her instincts were sending alarm bells: her baser instincts were dancing as she smiled inwardly and followed The Driver. Walking along the narrow path Laura observed the character of the cottage. It had a warm ambience all of its own. Nestled among a streetscape of traditional English-style gardens, the front entrance was devoted to roses of every combination all perfectly blending in colour and heady perfume. Painted in a soft hue of terracotta the house itself was of unusual design composed of mud-washed brick. It did not dominate its environment but seemed to be a part of it. Each direction you looked you could spot a sample of hand-hewn art - a pottery urn here, a metal sculpture there.

Inside, the cottage was sparsely furnished. Bare boards with woven rugs scattered strategically across the floors. Muted colours on the walls provided a backdrop for paintings, sculptures and wall hangings. An eclectic collection of cushions and easy chairs surrounded a finely carved coffee table which took pride of place in this large room. The place possessed a wonderful warmth and a spirit of belongingness.

"Scotch? Or would you prefer a wine?"

Caught mid-admiration of her surroundings, Laura answered vaguely. "What? Oh, I'd prefer a wine, thank you."

The Driver turned from the bar with a full glass extended toward her, raising an eyebrow as he asked mischievously, "And is that your only preference?"

Laura took in a sharp breath. She decided the game before was a skirmish and the real play was about to begin. Casting caution aside and following instincts was the only route left open to her in this new territory.

Slowly and deliberately, she asked, "How many times have you used this - *technique* - to lure women?"

The Driver sat near her with scotch in hand and looked sheepish. "Never. But I don't expect you'll believe me."

Laura was suddenly aware of a vulnerability in this person who had shown such control and confidence behind the wheel. She could perceive clearly the shift of power in the room from The Driver to herself. And the feeling of that felt unashamedly good to Laura.

Laura languidly lifted herself from the chaise lounge and unconsciously licked her top lip leisurely. She circled the lounge slowly.

The Driver seemed bemused. "By the way, I should introduce myself - name's Carl."

Staring silently out the window she said, "I know".

Carl spun his head in her direction.

"Oh yes, I know. But you don't know me. Of course I wasn't sure at first. Not until I saw your cufflinks."

It was only after Carl sat down near her that she saw the glint of the Maserati cufflinks, that unmistakable trident logo glistening in the incandescent light.

They were the same hallmark accessory she saw nearly every day when she was Temping at O'Donnell & Rodhich Legal. Carl would walk past her and if he didn't ignore her, would look down at her disdainfully. Laura overheard him in the lift one day not long before her Temp role abruptly ended. "… and get rid of that fat chick on Reception - it's not a good look for the firm having a smelly elephant as a first impression. I want someone on there a potential client wants to bed, not shoot for a trophy."

She savoured the confusion on Carl's face.

"You're attracted to me now, aren't you Carl? Think I'm worth a chase and a conquest? You didn't think so a couple of years ago. I was 120kgs heavier then. Remember the elephant on Reception?"

All Carl could do was stutter and look perplexed.

Bethany's words flashed into her mind - you've gotta grab what life puts in front of you.

"Imagine meeting you again like this, Carl. Shame it has to be so short."

Surprise was the last look to pass across Carl's face, as Laura pulled out her gleaming Beretta 92FS 9mm pistol and popped two bullets into him.

"Pity I can't take home a trophy." mused Laura.

Then she saw the Maserati cufflinks.

Faulty Weights and Measures

Lyndall Nairn

Keptie Street, Arbroath, Angus, Scotland, 1867

Standing on the footpath outside the Keptie Street grocery shop, the council inspector paused as he deposited the confiscated weights and measuring jugs into his cart. Who was to blame? The widow or the widower? The current proprietor, James Nairn, had seemed genuinely taken aback when the inspector pronounced that he was confiscating fifteen of the twenty-one weights and measures that he had tested that day. They were not correct, and James would have to replace them.

"You can't blame your customers for expecting a fair deal," the inspector had reminded him. "And the Council expects all shopkeepers in Angus to be honest in their trading."

James had nodded in agreement, but the inspector could tell from his expression that James was troubled.

"Ah, well," the inspector thought, "He's new to this work. Perhaps he thought he could get away with shaving a bit off the weights and increasing the thickness of the bottom of the measuring jugs." When they had shaken hands, the inspector had noticed the calluses on James' hand, a sign of the years he had spent as an agricultural labourer before moving into town to take over the grocery business that his second wife had inherited from her first husband. Then the inspector remembered that James' wife had been conspicuous by her absence while he was testing the weights and measures, an indication that she could be the guilty party.

Meanwhile, inside the shop, James ushered the last of his customers out of the shop, feeling embarrassed that they had witnessed the inspector confiscating so many of his weights and measures. He locked the door, turned the sign to "Closed", and stomped upstairs to find his wife.

Isabelle looked up, startled that her husband had left the shop. "Anything wrong?" she asked.

"Aye," James replied. "For the first time in my life, I've been accused of a crime. What's more, I've been found guilty."

He collapsed into a chair and covered his head with his hands.

"What's this? You're the last person to be committing crimes!"

"It's the weights and measures in the shop! The inspector tested twenty-one and found fifteen to be under, so he has taken them. Now we have to buy new ones.

How was I to know that we have been diddling our customers? Did this ever happen when William was in the shop?"

Isabelle looked at the floor. "Oh, once or twice, but it was never a big matter. You know, sometimes the weights and measures are not correct when we buy them. It's impossible to make them so precise all the time."

"But this was not one or two! The inspector took fifteen! And you can't blame the manufacturers. Isabelle, what more can you tell me?"

"Oh, I don't know! After William died, it was all so difficult! I didn't have enough help, and some things in the shop were neglected. Perhaps I wasn't careful enough about cleaning the weights and measuring jugs."

"Hmmph." James realised that he had just heard the closest thing to a confession that his wife could come up with, but she was quick to put her contrition behind her.

"Besides," she said, adopting a lighter tone, "Having a few weights confiscated doesn't make you a criminal. It's not as if you're a convict about to be transported to New South Wales!"

James gave her a begrudging smile, but as he went downstairs to re-open the shop, he decided that never again would the inspector find any reason to take any of his weights and measures.

Source: Angus County Archives, Forfar, Angus, Scotland. Report by the Dean of Guild on Weights and Measures of Arbroath. 1864, William Dorward, Keptie Street, p. 45; 1867, James Nairn, Keptie Street, p.96; 1868, James Nairn, Keptie Street, p. 134.

Nothing to See Here

Ken Brown

The smell was clogging up my throat and nose. It was gut-wrenchingly vomit-inducing and almost visible in the humid early morning air. The coroner's man was grinning at me like some dick from a locked sectioned ward.

"Have a closer look", he said motioning at the newly opened grave, "you have to look, and don't spew last night's cocoa over what's left of him."

The ropes were pulling up what was left of a coffin and placing it down near me. It had ruptured so the smell was now overpowering.

"Cheap bastards," exclaimed the man operating the ropes, "a coffin like this doesn't last long."

By now I was going to faint, and the coroner's man told me to look away as the lid came off. Flies everywhere. Grave diggers, unperturbed, were smoking and gossiping alongside the rotted wooden box.

"Let's have a bit of him" the coroner called out, "no need to take everything back to the slab.

It was Friday and my hangover was sad and bad.

Let's go back to Monday morning at the police HQ.

"Come in here," called my inspector. "Close the door."

Oh, Christ, I thought, another frigging lecture. I was partly wrong. The inspector didn't ask me to take a seat but just waved a sheaf of paperwork at me.

"This is an order from the health department allowing the coroner to exhume Larry Murdoch from his pit and reopen the inquest into his death, and you need to be there to witness the removal. His brother has been haunting the fucking government to reopen the case. Get down there Friday and ask questions of his last known next of kin."

"What did the coroner's report state"? I asked.

"Open verdict and try not to spend much time on this late piece of shite," the inspector replied.

"Before you go, Angus, I just have to say I can't wait for you to die or quit after 28 years. I used to like you when we were young cops starting out, but you never got past constable and became an oxygen bandit years ago. You are a fucking disgrace, now piss off and report back within a week."

It's true, I am a failure at policing and life in general. To add to my problems, I am quite short for a copper, so few took me seriously. No one to mourn me in my final hours. The doctor told me with a sense of triumph, "you have advanced liver and kidney failure caused mainly by heavy and persistent drinking."

It was hardly surprising – I was rapidly getting cheaper grog for dinner and breakfast. At forty-eight I was just about gone and didn't care.

Anyway, back to Larry Murdoch. After witnessing the retrieval, I hid in the long grass covering an old grave and vomited. I was not happy. And neither was the ground keeper.

My enquiries took me to his widow, name of Ann.

"What do you want now?" she yelled at me, "he just upped and died overnight and no reason given, and I couldn't care less then or now, so stop talking to me and fuck off!"

"One last question" I casually said, "where was your daughter, Emma when Larry died"?

"Here in bed, what did you lot expect, she was only twelve, and he had given me a right hiding for not having any drink in the house. Didn't make much difference as he was nearly on the floor already."

"It says here your daughter was seeing a boy at the time. Know where he is now?" I said to an already closing door.

"Try the caravan park!" was the helpful answer.

Arriving at the park I enquired at the shack that was shyly pretending to be an office about anyone there called Emma.

"First caravan on your left and remind them about the rent."

Emma was there together with an older fellow. What struck me was that this bloke, was in fine muscular shape and as they say "ripped."

He told me he was Trevor.

"Emma," I began, "what do you remember about the night your stepdad died?"

"Jeeze!" she spat it out. "don't you bastards ever give up?"

"Where were you, Trevor?" I asked. I may be a failure as a copper, but I can still know when someone is lying or hiding something.

"Mind if I look inside" I casually asked pushing past the pair.

"Can we stop you?" replied Emma.

"Not people like you," I said and immediately regretted saying it.

Inside, the place stank of fags and sweat. Trevor seemed anxious. I spotted a box of syringes and had a look. Insulin and lots of it. I regretted not having a search warrant.

"Are these yours, Trevor? Are you a diabetic?"

"No" he replied.

"Then why?" I asked.

"At the gym we and me mates and me try to become not just huge but humongous and we inject insulin to drive sugar from our muscles. To get ripped. You have to be fucking careful because insulin will quickly kill you if used too much and without supervision. Will take just a few hours."

"Were you sleeping with Emma the night Larry died"? I asked.

"Course I was, to protect her from her old man I was."

"An underage girl," I gently reminded him, "so tell me what you did on that night, and did you have insulin in your possession?"

Emma screamed at me to just leave it be, but I persisted promising to arrest Trevor for underage sex if he didn't cooperate.

Emma seemed to collapse and told me that she was terrified at what Larry would do to her mother as he had battered her badly a week before. She had looked up insulin on a friend's phone and found that all traces disappeared from the body some hours after death.

"Me and Trev got all the stuff and kept injecting it in his gut and then threw all the needles away. We couldn't take it any longer he wouldn't leave, and mum loved him."

"So, is that why no one called the police until some hours later in the day - to cover up?" I said.

By now both Trevor and Emma were sobbing about jail and withdrawal symptoms.

I walked outside and pondered my duty.

"Don't forget the rent," I called as I got back into my car.

After a respectable interval, the coroner again pronounced nothing new to see and formally closed the case. I went to my inspector and told him it was probably the grog that took Larry and no point in stirring up more enquiries. The inspector told me that this was a satisfying conclusion for all and if I didn't put in my papers, he would get me sacked.

Going out into the warm sunshine I had only two thoughts. One was *who will I leave my super payout to* and the other *I was glad to have finally done some good for a couple of wasters not dissimilar to myself.*

The pains were getting much worse.

I probably shouldn't be driving.

Old Walters Apples

Gloria Buchanan

Could this be the same place? I had followed the dusty track down from the main road. The water covered where the cabin and the horse paddock had been. The creek is now part of the lake. I walked on up the hill gingerly crossing a tangled barbed wire fence and stumbled across an old stone chimney covered in lantana. Was this where Old Walter's house had stood?

Old Walter was Dad's father - us kids always called him *Old Walter* as he said he was nobody's grandfather. He and Dad did not get along, some quarrel from years ago. Old Walter was a mean codger who had a great garden and orchard. He didn't share his produce though, sold it all at his little roadside stall up on the highway, nothing off his trees for the local kids. Times were tough. Dad worked hard as a fisherman out in his boat day and night whenever the fish were on. The family lived in a small cabin on the bank of the creek.

Jim and I had been sneaking into old Walter's orchard for a week. Climbing over the barbed wire fence, keeping an eye out for his two rottweilers, real savage they were. He often sat in his old rocking chair on his front veranda looking out for those 'rotten thieves.' If he wasn't there, we knew he was out and it was safe to do a little scavenging, except for the dogs of course. The apples were a little green as we found out to our discomfort. Mum said they were just right for cooking. Jim and I had been gorging ourselves on apple pies - even Dad enjoyed them. Maybe he thought his father had given them to us. As if that was likely. Mum found the tomatoes that followed us home very handy. Did she know where they came from? She didn't ask and we didn't tell her.

We hadn't been to his garden for a few days when one afternoon after school Jim gives me this sly grin.

'I hear Old Walters melons are getting ripe I'm sure the stingy old bugger won't give us any. He wouldn't miss one he has got so many.' Jim decided it was worth one more foray into the orchard.

We waited till just on dark the next night. Things would have been peachy if only Jim's old dog Cleopatra had stayed home. Jim's fault, he should have tied her up. Jim and I climbed over the fence with no trouble. We were looking for a nice ripe melon and whatever else we could find. We were making our way back when Cleopatra started barking. Those two rottweilers came down from the house flat out and did we take off. It could have been curtains for us. Those dogs were making a terrible racket - we made it to the fence just in time. I must say we were a little hampered by the watermelon I was carrying, and Jim had two rock melons under his arms as well as apples up his shirt. The light flared from the veranda - we could hear Old Walter yelling and swearing.

'I know who you are you little thieves,' he roared as he fired a volley of bird shot over our heads.

Mum found out the next day when old Walter came to the house raging and cursing.

'You need to do something about your thieving sons. Keep them off my property or I'll report them to the police.'

Mum promptly forgot about the fruit and veggies we had been providing. I really think she took old Walter's threats seriously. Did we cop a thrashing. Jim was not happy.

'I'm gonna teach him a lesson. If he wasn't such a skinflint, I'd just cop the beating.'

'Watch yuh gonna do?

'You'll find out. best you don't know,' was all he would say.

Jim was on his best behaviour, but I knew he was just biding his time.

"Bad weather coming boys,' Dad warned us.' Stay out of the bush, trees can come down in a strong wind.'

That night it was very black, the crack of thunder, the howling of the wind muffling all sound. The rain was pounding on the corrugated iron roof. I saw Jim creeping out through the night. Flashes of lightning shining on the saw in his hand. He returned before dawn, drenched.

'Where have you been,' I whispered.

'Never you mind,' was all he said.

'Old Walter is on the rampage,' Dad said when he came in from checking his boat the next morning.

'Apparently, he lost a good few of his apple trees, came down in the storm. It was just bad luck but of course, he is saying it's sabotage. Reckons he is going to the police. Constable Jones won't do anything he is sick of his complaints. Serves him right, he is always blaming someone for stealing something.'

That had been so long ago. All were gone now. The Lake Munmorah Power Station and lake covered all the familiar sites.

I can still see Jim's silly grin that day. Old Walter never did find out what happened to his trees, but we stayed well away from his orchard for quite a while.

The Experiment

Dianne Keogh

Professor Markham visibly shook as he reinspected the student's radar images more closely. Jean-Pierre sat silently waiting for his grade. Without a word, the Professor ran urgently out of his office and headed for the archeology department. *I hope this doesn't mean what I think it means*! shaking his head in disbelief.

The images were part of an experiment by his third-year Physics students using ground-penetrating radar. A simple experiment in the outer fields of the old Kinross School. The site was now owned by the Council, who had recently transformed it into a museum, and it had proven to be a very popular attraction for locals and tourists alike. The images showed reflections produced by graves, evenly spaced, of consistent size and at regular spacings. This was going to be big; he could just feel it.

***

The local newsroom was jumping as the afternoon deadline fast approached. Adriel sat at his desk looking dreamily out the window, then violently stubbed out his cigarette.

A small flock of pigeons gathered nervously on the window ledge and he regarded them with curiosity. A large storm cloud approached from the west and reminded him of his childhood story on the Reservation about the mysterious Thunderbird. A mythical creature with dual personalities. It could be both a grandfather or a terrorizer, beating its wings and flashing its eyes violently to change the weather. It may bring tornadoes and rain to restore nature's order or be a portend of disaster. Which was it today? he mused. An intriguing story of a primeval Life Force that could kill, or bring the world back to a happier place.

Suzanne, one of the other journalists, suddenly appeared at his desk, fanning a crumpled envelope under his nose. It was marked urgent, confidential and addressed to him personally. She stood watching inquisitively while he opened and read the note, which was written in poorly scrawled handwriting. The writer asked Adriel to meet him at the old Kinross school and was signed, Stan, The Gardener. Interesting. Earlier that morning he had received a tip-off from his insider contact at the police that there had been some unusual findings uncovered by university students at the school last week.

***

Adriel spotted Stan, the Gardener, the moment he drove into the school grounds. He was waiting on the porch, easily recognizable by his clothing and the rake he lent on. The site buzzed with activity and was littered with police cars, flashing lights and yellow crime tape. Numerous Detectives were busily interviewing staff.

Stan was in his early seventies with a serious demeanour, but his kind, mischievous blue eyes belied a man with a keen sense of humour. He gestured Adriel to follow him into a small shed at the back of the main building and dragged a large, heavy tin box down from high above on a shelf.

Opening the tin, Adriel found it full of photographs and documents. The photographs were of young children, standing orderly having their photos taken, with the school building in the backdrop. Hundreds of young Native American children appeared in the photos and they were surrounded by Brothers, Seminarians and a few Nuns. The children looked austere and unhappy, and the staff stern and supercilious. These must have been terrible times for the young children just starting out their lives.

Stan told Adriel the police had found 248 graves in the outer fields of the school, the bodies of small Native American children, some still dressed in their school clothes. Adriel felt sick and drained. He stumbled, leaning against a wooden bench in the workroom, almost falling. He was numb. This was horrendous. Forensics had estimated the graves were at least fifty years old. Adriel was speechless. Stan said the story needed to be told and offered Adriel exclusive access to the photos and records in the box. He explained that he had found this box a few months ago during routine maintenance work at the edge of the forest tree line but had kept its existence to himself.

'I was a young man when I started working here.' Stan explained. 'The Church ran the school and the Brothers and Seminarians were the teaching staff. There were a few nuns, though they kept quietly to themselves, attending mainly to the chores of feeding and clothing the children'.

Adriel saw the pain in Stan's eyes as he recounted his first days on the job as a Cleaner and how inhumanely the children were treated. He later joined the Army and said he served with Native American servicemen and he felt ashamed that he had not alerted the authorities at the time to what had been going on at the school. After the Army, he returned to work at the school as a Gardener for the next 20 years and the school then had less children. He explained that he had no idea about the massacre that had occurred there all those decades ago.

The names of staff and the dates the photos were taken were written clearly on the back of each photograph. Adriel stood frozen in the shed and his first thought was how this would impact his Native American community.

Adriel felt compelled to promptly consult his Elders and receive guidance on his duty and responsibilities as a member of their community.

Stan was clearly upset and the tears welled deep in his crystal blue eyes. The two men stood silently together sharing a deep moment of solemn silence and reflection. He shook hands with Stan and the two men embraced.

Adriel left, urgent to interview the police outside.

Adriel's mind was racing with the implications of this find and the story. Evil just never seems to go away, it keeps coming back. It never dies…. Many healing ceremonies would follow and the community would be in deep grief for a long time, maybe forever. This was a big responsibility to cover the story but he did have a job to keep and as long as he covered it sensitively and followed Elders' advice, he would be alright. It was important. He decided that he would write the story.

***

The songs from the conspiracy of robins were deafening. Robins, some cultures believed, were messengers, a sign of angels and the loving heart, and that loved ones are at peace or visiting them. Father Ryan sat alone on the garden bench in the sweeping, beautiful gardens soaking up the warm sun on his face as it beat down on him. It was May, and Spring was here. All was lovely and green.

He turned the note over and over in his hands. *I know what you have done,* it read. He could instantly recall the faces of the little Native American Indian children innocently begging him for mercy. He remembered the great sense of power he felt. It had rushed through his veins with excitement. He felt absolute power, an enormous strength, as he gave the order for the weak ones to be buried in the field. There were hundreds of them buried that year.

As he stuffed the note violently into his pocket, a small, light feather floated out from the envelope. He swiped at it with disdain as it floated down lightly and away. He walked slowly back to the sitting room of his retirement home. Head held high and proud. He didn't care. No one knew. No one cared. It was a long time ago. He was invincible, unchallenged, untouchable. Well, until now. He flicked a beetle off his coat and stomped his right foot hard down on it, squishing it beyond recognition.

As he sat reading in the sitting room of his retirement home, he heard the sirens screaming urgently in the distance and within minutes the Emergency Response Team flooded the grounds. He looked out the window. They were coming for him. He knew it. They had discovered his toys, for that's all they were, meaningless toys to play with, to amuse him and his staff. He was resigned to his fate. Prison - well that will be amusing, for sure. Bring it on. He smiled and returned to reading his book. His face wore a smirk and he slumped back in his chair arrogant, relaxed and entitled.

Red Roses for Your Coffin

Jeannie Bennett

His hot breath brushed the back of her neck. This time he was close. He'd followed her home from work before but always from a distance. The night was dark. Clouds smothered the moon and winter fog shrouded Barker Street in Redbrook. Out of breath, Emma concentrated on the path ahead. Her heart was thumping in her chest. He whispered.

'I'll get you soon.'

His hands grabbed at her jacket. One covered her mouth. The other pulled her close. His breath smelled sweet.

'I'll let you go, Emma. Our time together later will be all the sweeter for waiting.'

Emma raced home. After she locked the door and windows she fell to the floor and tears coursed down her cheeks.

Her mobile rang but Emma couldn't move to answer it. The second time she heard it, she saw her mother's number come up.

'The creep again. He caught me this time but let me go.' Emma could hardly talk. 'I froze inside again and couldn't move to defend myself.'

'Please ring the police right now, Emma.' Her mother pleaded. 'I heard on the News again about the "Roses rapist in Redbrook" who always leaves red roses for his victims before he strangles them. I can't lose you!'

'I called them the last time he followed me, and a policeman said he'd send an officer around. No one came. I reckon they thought I was making it up.'

'Ring them again! I know you don't trust policemen; they didn't even charge your ex when he bashed you up last year, but most of them are good. You need help, Emma.'

'They blamed me, Mum. Remember, he was a policeman too. I'll call them if anything else happens.'

Her mum pleaded with her again and reminded her of the drama production, "Ginger" that Emma had played a lead role in the previous year. Emma came alive with a plan which included calling the police first thing in the morning.

In the middle of the night, the doorbell woke Emma from one nightmare to another. She peeked through the glass but could see no one at the front door in the fog. On her step lay three bunches of glorious red roses.

Memories of the night before crowded into her brain. Her body trembled as she opened the door and picked up the closest bunch of roses.

Emma gasped as she read the message on the card.

Happy death day, Emma.

These roses will decorate your coffin at

Your funeral, scheduled tomorrow, 26th June 2019

At Redbrook Crematorium where

The flames will lick and consume your body.

Emma screamed as she slammed the door and locked it. She needed help. She groped for her phone to call Triple Zero then yelled 'Help, help!' as the doorbell peeled again. She saw a shadow looming beside the front door.

'It's the police here, Emma.' The doorknob jiggled a little.

Emma hesitated then opened the door a crack. The uniformed policeman put one foot in the opening. He flashed a badge in front of her.

'I heard you scream, Emma. Tell me what happened. I'll take all the details from you and follow it up.'

Emma showed him the flowers and the card. She described the times she was sure someone had followed her home from work. She gulped and trembled as he pushed the door open and walked in. She felt dwarfed by his presence and her courage slid away.

'Sit down, Emma, and try to settle yourself. Can you describe the man?' He removed his policeman's hat and sat at her table. Emma tried to picture the stalker and remembered his large body and hands when he came close to her the previous night. He pulled a bag of sweets from his pocket and offered her one.

'They're Turkish Delights, made from rosewater. Don't you just love the smell, Emma?' The policeman popped one in his mouth and she smelled the sweetness she'd smelled last night. Emma startled and struggled to reply.

'Ginger.' She croaked. "I prefer ginger. No, I didn't see him.' She'd only heard a swear word last night and it had been too dark to see him. She couldn't identify the stalker, but could the policeman be the man who'd followed her? A pine table stood between him and her. She cursed herself for not calling for help before.

The room was closing in on her and her heart pounded. Dizziness threatened to envelop her. His dark eyes stared directly into her blue ones and then locked onto her body, across from his. She focussed on her experience with the local drama production where she'd played "Ginger", a potential murder victim like she was now. She remembered how she'd learned to think and feel like a survivor, not a victim. She'd practised to keep her face free from emotion and speak as if she wasn't terrified. In the play, she'd found the role challenging and worked for long hours with coaching from the producer and her psychologist to convince the audience and herself. Emma had accepted the role, determined to overcome the fear engendered by her abusive experiences with her ex-boyfriend and took it up again now to survive. Could she apply the training to this life-and-death situation?

Her thoughts centred in her brain. The word "Ginger" emerged and repeated, inspiring her to follow her plan from the previous night. Once again, she made herself "Ginger", determined to survive, not to be raped or strangled. She looked at the enemy beast across the table and suggested

'I'll put the coffee maker on and bring us both a mug after I visit the bathroom. That'll help me settle a bit. Do you take sugar or milk?' The man leant back in his chair; he seemed in no hurry.

'Milk and two sugars.'

Emma still had her phone in her hand. She willed her feet to walk slowly and took some deep breaths. She switched the coffee maker on and then headed to the ensuite inside her bedroom. She reviewed her plan in silence.

'Lock the bedroom door, push the pink bedroom chair against the door, then the second. Grab the knife and the baseball bat from under my pillow. Lock the ensuite door and phone triple Zero.'

The chairs were heavy, but terror fuelled Emma's body and she tipped the second one upside down on top of the first. She heard the kitchen chair squeak as he stood up, he was coming for her.

No time to think, she locked herself in the ensuite and dialled Triple 0. She turned and caught sight of herself in the mirror; she looked like a ghost in her white flannelette pyjamas with her red curly hair sticking up and her blue eyes huge in her bloodless face. Anger set in. Another man wrecking her life! It was time to help herself.

As she fought dizziness, she heard the responder say, 'Take a deep breath, Emma and tell me your address. Are you in immediate danger?' Emma gave her address, then pleaded in panic.

'Yes! Stalker in my flat – I'm in the ensuite – help now!'

'Help is on the way, Emma. Is there a window you can climb out?'

Emma looked up. The only window was too tiny for her to fit through and too high for her to access.

His voice called through the bedroom door. 'Where's my coffee, Emma?' She heard a crash and then he knocked on the ensuite door. 'I'm waiting for you and looking forward to our time together. We need to decide how to arrange the roses. Is red your favourite colour?' At the word "red", she remembered the red sauce for blood she'd spread around the rubber knife in the drama production and grabbed the knife handle ready to make her attacker suffer. Emma sank to the floor next to the toilet.

The ensuite door gave way as he crowed like a rooster at dawn.

'Where are you, Emma?' He bent down to grab her. Emma shrank back. He turned to the right, his left thorax open to her. She thrust the knife up and in. He hit out. She pushed. This blade was sharp, not black rubber like in the play. Red blood splattered. Ginger jabbed again. He squealed. She twisted the knife – as hard as she could. He floundered to grab her. Sirens shrilled.

Four policemen and three paramedics crowded into the flat, but Emma's mother squeezed through them and bashed the bloodied man with her handbag.

The news that night was titled "Redbrook Rapist caught with red roses in his hands."

Emma was determined to stop the rapes and murders and followed legal advice. She and her mother supported

each other in counselling, but she would never have red
roses in the house again.

Snowy and the Map

Tom Penrose

Edward 'Snowy' White and Jack 'Fingers' Fuller waited in the queue to go through the security x-ray at the airport. No talking where they could be overheard. They negotiated the machine and emerged in the departure lounge. To anyone seeing them, they could be two well-dressed businessmen travelling to an important meeting, but appearances can be deceiving. The shorter man, Snowy, had recently been released from prison for his part in a Post Office robbery. As the driver of the getaway car, Snowy had received a lesser sentence than the men who carried out the heist. His travelling companion was well known to the police as a professional pickpocket, hence his nickname, 'Fingers'.

They wandered past the newsagent selling tacky Australian souvenirs and the Aussie clothing shop trying to flog cheap outback clothing and hats to Asian tourists, through the 'International' Food Hall selling hamburgers and sushi and found their way to a deserted departure gate where they could talk and not worry about being heard.

'Didn't think you liked flying,' said Fingers.

'I don't,' returned Snowy, 'but it's the fastest way of getting to the Island, and we haven't got a lot of time. Mad Dog is not the patient type.'

'It's only a short flight mate. Went out there last month like you asked, had a bit of a sniff around. Gees, it's taken off in the last few years, you wouldn't know the place. Real tourist trap now, new airport, new hotels. Getting some cheap digs wasn't easy, they all want to charge like wounded bulls.'

'Don't worry too much about money. Once we get our hands on the cash we'll be set.'

'You were lucky Mad Dog trusted you with the map.'

'He knows I wouldn't double-cross him.'

'Bloody truth is you wouldn't double-cross him and live.'

'Yeah, well that may be so, but I promised to take just my cut and drop the rest off to his wife, and I plan to do just that. There will be enough for us.'

'Thanks for asking me to help.'

'Well, it wouldn't have looked good for me to be going around buying picks and shovels and things, would it?'

'No, I guess not. I've got them all stored in one of those storage sheds, but I didn't know where we'd be digging so I had to take a chance with which one I picked. Anyway, I've hired a car so we can move them around tonight.'

'Okay,' said Snowy. 'I can give you a quick squizz at the map and we can work out the loggergistics.'

Fingers smiled but he knew what Snowy meant.

Snowy took a small sheet of folded paper from his pocket and handed it to Fingers.

Fingers unfolded the map and sat speechless for a second, he then looked up at Snowy.

'Bloody hell mate, you buried it right under the middle of the new airport runway.'

The Butler Did It

Louie Page

'Speech! Speech, Detective Albright', the crowd cheered.

Yes, well, that would be me. I would like to say thank you all for attending my retirement after 40 years in the force, working my way through the ranks. I am not one for long speeches, but we worked cases as a team and put in hundreds of hours to solve each case. But there comes a time when I must hang up my hat and retire. Thank you for all the memories.

Our newest detective rookie, Andrew, has asked me to pick out the most memorable case I have ever worked. In the background, people cry out, "the Butler did it."

The first case that I solved as a detective. Brilliant work to all of you that were there but what you don't know is I had a secret helper.

The crowd looked to each other in wonder. What did he mean?

It was the most bizarre case to figure out. Who killed Mr. Butler. Now I really do feel like an old man telling a bunch of blokes a bedtime story. Grab your drinks and I will tell you what happened on that cold Saturday evening, April 1st, 1995.

High in the hills lived the Butler family, in the quiet village of Whatsup. A small community with a population of about 300. Everybody knows everyone and strange things rarely happen. Mr. Butler was well known to the community as he was the sole owner of an Australian Real Estate Company, worth billions. Mr. Butler invested millions into the property market spread across Australia. His family lived all over the country. His philanthropic investments were orphanages, wellness centres, hospitals, and retreats for the sick and injured. Regardless, he was a generous gentleman, with a big heart for the greater good. I knew him in my younger years and remembered Mr. Butler always smoked Cuban cigars and drank scotch on the rocks. The odd part was the ice was always circle-shaped not cubed. How do you make ice balls? The crowd laughed.

The immediate family received an invitation to the celebration of their parent's 40th wedding anniversary. There was another letter attached informing the family about changes to his Will. Each family member was to choose a charitable organisation to donate their inheritance to. On the letter it said his lawyer will be there to officially sign the necessary changes. The family was to meet in the library at ten pm.

The Butler family consisted of three sons: Barron the eldest at thirty, a veterinarian. Philip was twenty-seven and trained in toxicology and their youngest Aaron was twenty-five, a computer programmer. His family wanted for nothing; they lived in million-dollar mansions in prime locations across Australia. They had holiday homes, luxury boats and cars as well as extremely healthy bank accounts.

For the special occasion, Mrs. Butler had the mansion decorated in a classy manner. The mansion had pools, tennis courts and a helicopter pad. She had also arranged ten butlers, fifteen waiters and ten famous chefs to prepare and serve food fit for the celebration. Overall, one hundred and fifty-five people were attending. All dressed up in a gala evening dress. There were men in penguin suits with tails and waiters wore white cotton gloves.

Earlier in the evening, Mr. Butler experienced chest pains and his pilot had flown him to hospital in his helicopter. About thirty minutes later, we received an anonymous call announcing he was dead on arrival. This was suspicious considering the changes to the Will. It became our top priority case, as millions were at stake and his death was so sudden. The party continued as per Mr. Butler's last instructions.

A doctor told the family of Mr. Butler passing. The family gathered their emotions and decided that Mrs. Butler would make an announcement to the guests as the event had taken a sombre turn and had turned into a celebration of life. 'The police are here requesting your details as this is the usual protocol. Our apologies for the inconvenience but as my now late husband had requested, the party must go on' said Mrs. Butler holding back the tears behind a tissue.

My first priority as the detective in charge was taking statements from each member of the family. Each one had a reason to kill him due to the Will changes, the hard part was 'who killed the Butler?'

Sitting in their fancy lounge in the large library, I was looking at the new Will, at the chosen charities that the sons had decided to donate their inheritance to and was surprised that Mrs. Butler was also required to donate her inheritance. His death now made these documents null and void.

That was when I received the first anonymous call on my mobile phone. I answered and the voice on the other end sounded obscured saying 'look to your right, the bookcase moves'. The call ended. I walked over and found a button. A secret passageway opened and then automatically closed. Inside was a layout of ten computer screens with three chairs. The late Mr. Butler had serious security concerns. There was a camera in each room angled to see everyone. On the desk was a floppy disc that said, 'Play Me.' I sat down and inserted the disc into the computer. It dated 31st March 1995 and showed Barron Butler, the veterinarian, injecting some kind of vile liquid into one cigar and replacing the now toxic

Cuban cigar back into the box. He had made a mark on the gold wrap that was obvious to him and him alone. 'Gotcha' I said. I grabbed my radio and instructed the police officers to collect all the cigars boxes and bag & tag them. Also, hunt down any cigars that are in the ashtrays, label and send them all to the lab for any traces of toxins that Mr. Butler may have inhaled that could cause his sudden death.

My phone rang again. The same obscured voice said 'Detective Albright as you can see, I am helping you in this investigation however, if you share this with a single soul your creditability will be destroyed as a Detective. Do we have an agreement? I gave the caller my word. 'But we have Barron Butler possibly killing Mr. Butler with whatever he injected into his cigar.' 'Detective Albright, we have just begun. Now take the disc out and place it into your right-hand pocket. Go to the first computer and press enter.'

Dated 1st of April 3.18 pm, I was watching the screen, seeing Philip dressed as a waiter wearing white cotton gloves, crushing shards of glass in a pestle and mortar, then scooping it up and placing it into half circle ice cube trays. The lookalike waiter then carefully placed the trays into the freezer, looked at his watch and walked out of the door.

I radioed my police officers and ordered them to go and bag and tag the round ice trays and let me know if any ice was left in them. It didn't take long before an officer said, 'yes, there are two trays of circle-shaped ice cubes in the freezer with a few ice balls left.' I instructed them to put the trays in a sealed box but leave them in the freezer for now.' When they are sent to the lab, ask them to check for crushed glass.

My phone rang once more. The same voice said 'go out to look around for yourself Detective Albright, and let your team know that you still exist as you've been busy. People are wondering what you have been doing and we both agreed we do not want suspicions raised now. I walked downstairs. By this time, it was still early, and the guests had moved to the east wing of the mansion, continuing to celebrate Mr. Butler's life. Drinking and reminiscing while looking over photo albums, chatting with each other.

Walking towards the master bedroom, I came across Sergeant Hint. He showed me a handkerchief that had blood splattered on it. 'I found this on Mr. Butler's side of the bed, and it looks to me like it's from coughing. I thought Mr. Butler was having chest pains, not coughing blood. What do you make it?'

Take it to the lab and compare the D.N.A. with Mr. Butler. I entered their ensuite where the medicine cabinet had bottles for Mr. Butler's heart condition and instructions for his pacemaker. Mrs. Butler was on

Valium. I noted the date was one week ago but there were only two remaining tablets. I asked the police officer to make a record of all the medications and remove one tablet of each, test it, to make sure the substance is as described, a standard procedure. Fingerprints as well.

From there I walked in and out of their three sons' bedrooms looking at their trophies, awards and certificates hung on the walls. All have the ability to get away with murder. I patted my pocket, and the disc was not there. 'Damn, I muttered to myself, got balls to steal off a cop.' Down the hallway was Aaron's room. There were certificates everywhere, mostly computer awards. In a frame there was a high school suspension statement for hacking into the school's computer files and changing his grades to overachiever with credits.

My phone rang. 'Where is the floppy disc? I need that, it is evidence of this investigation' I asked the now familiar voice.

'Detective, impatience is a virtue', the scrambled voice answered.

'Return to the security room I have a gift for you.'

Not once did it cross my mind that this person was here. I was looking around while I headed to the secret entry and sure enough there on the desk was another floppy disc. The date - 1st April at 6.35 pm Aaron, a whiz with computers, he was typing what looked to me like medical documents I pressed pause, for a closer look. Aaron was changing what looked like the medical setting on Mr. Butlers pacemaker. The screen went blank. That was no coincidence, that at the same time that Mr. Butler felt unwell, and his doctor transported him to the hospital on the chopper.

Heading out of the security room with my hand on the doorknob. Something caught my eye when a screen flashed the date 20th March 10.46 am, which was over a week ago. The camera was recording Mrs. Butler in the medicine cabinet looking for a particular bottle, turning them around looking at the labels. She put ten capsules aside into another container, then she emptied the remaining capsule powder in the sink. She began filling them up with a white powder from a container that she pulled out of her pocket. She wiped her fingerprints off the container and flushed the medicine down the drain. Looked in the mirror, smiled at her reflection, before walking out.

My phone rang again. The same voice instructed me that I had a visitor waiting in the library. I entered the library to see the back of a gentleman who looked familiar, but I could not be certain. Mr. Butler turned towards me. I stood there in awe. 'It is the point of who did not try and kill you, sir. But seeing you are alive, I do have evidence to prove that all your family will be spending time in prison for attempted murder.'

'Excellent work detective, and I hear that this is your debut case. Well done.'

It is almost ten pm. Could you gather my family and request them to meet here please detective, then arrest them all and escort them out. I need them to see me sign the paperwork.'

I was sitting there in the library, and I asked Mr. Butler 'how did you know that your family would try and kill you?

'Greed' he replied. 'My wife surprised me though with the tablets she swapped.

Without my proper medication, I would have died five days ago.'

I shared with him the contents were now confirmed as plain salt.

Mr. Butler laughed, 'that would have made me thirsty, and I would have drunk more scotch. My son Philip put snake venom into my scotch. Horrible way to go, it slowly paralyses your body until all the organs shuts down.'

'Dreadful Mr. Butler, I did not see that on your computer.'

'How could you detective, as I have not told you where the security room is yet. There is only one person who knows about my secret security room, and you are looking at him. So, detective, you will need to organise a computer person to access the CCTV footage. I have notes here to help them with dates and times.

I said 'Thank you for your phone calls, Mr. Butler. It is the fastest open and closed murder case in history!'

'What phone calls are you referring detective? I have been watching my family having a wonderful time at the party. This is the first conversation we have had.'

A voice in the crowd cried out 'did you find out who was the anonymous caller?'

'I have always thought it was Mr. Butler as he said no one knew about the room. To this day, I do not know who helped me in this case, but I am grateful for the help.' As for Mr. Butler, he continued donating his fortune until the day he really died and gave his jailed family no further thought. I did receive a further gift from the anonymous caller a few days later. It was a floppy disk that simply said, 'play me.'

The Daisy Plains Gazette

Janice McLachlan

Lucy was a spinster. Not one of the tight-lipped, black-clad matrons that the epitaph usually evinced, but a colourful, willowy, bird of a woman, unperturbed by the privations of life.

The neighbourhood children tore barefoot through her house, helping themselves to freshly baked scones and homemade lemonade on the way. They climbed the sprawling Oaks in her yard to plank platforms and cubbies with rope swings. She adored them all and they adored her in return.

To do her part, as an upright member of her local community, Lucy edited the Daisy Plains Gazette, just a few pages, once a month, of interest only to a few. She wouldn't have admitted as much openly, but in truth, it was a bit of a bore. Each month, she struggled to fill even three pages with news, badgering friends for contributions, begging for advertisements to cover the cost of publication, pestering the best cooks for recipes, adding photos of the children and their creations, but little of interest happened in Daisy Plains.

So, Lucy started a monthly lady's lunch, a harmless gossip-fest, just bring a plate and something to drink and have a good time. With any luck, the talk might elicit content for the Gazette. There was a table in the deep shade of her favourite tree and a wicker basket full of toys for the children. She regularly scoured the op-shops for these offerings.

Each month, on the day set aside for the Gazette, Lucy rose early, positive affirmations on her tongue. She'd be grateful for a recipe, a weather report or even something rehashed from the Daily News, anything to add a little spice to the publication. No matter how often she told herself not to hope for too much, she couldn't still a thrill of anticipation as she saw the mailman coming up the lane, and then one day, she skipped down the path to find a nondescript envelope with the word Gazette glued to the front, being fingered by the inquisitive mailman. A tingle flew up Lucy's arms and her heart began to race. The envelope had a tantalising bulge. Surely it contained more than a single recipe. She was hardly game to open it. She told herself she was being silly. She'd been disappointed by junk mail before. She tried to restrain her enthusiasm but even junk mail was a welcome distraction.

Lucy nodded to the mailman, who raised one quizzical eyebrow, but she tucked the little envelope under her arm and marched, if not sedately at least with some decorum, back up the path and into her kitchen where, holding her breath and crossing her fingers, she tore at the envelope and poured its contents onto the table.

For a heartbeat, all she could do was stare. Then she gasped and then she giggled. She was not naturally unkind or excessively gossipy when measured with the yardstick of her ilk, but the frisson of excitement she experienced was like a shot in the arm to a heroin addict.

Sally's husband, Terry, was a crossdresser. He looked wonderful in pink, better than his wife, and there he was in all his glory, wearing pearls and heels and a feather in his hair. It was priceless.

At first, she wasn't sure she should publish but who would it hurt? Perhaps a few would suffer the slings and arrows of outrage or embarrassment, but life in such a staid little community held so little excitement, it was impossible to resist. It wasn't as if there were any doubt of the note's veracity. There was a picture in corroboration.

After publication, the next lady's lunch was a riotous affair. Wine flowed freely and gossip ran amuck. Sally shrugged off the attention with a wink and a giggle and the conversation turned to the author of the intelligence. Was it one of them and who would be next on centre stage? After all, they each had their own little foibles. Under the influence of the wine, they dared each other to greater excesses, promising to dress up in their husband's clothes. Even the children plunged into the spirit, wearing their mother's beads and feathers in their hair. The ladies were entranced. Lucy was a hero and Sally basked in the spotlight of their attention. But, as with all good things, it couldn't last, and life eventually returned to normal.

That was when the second little missive arrived.

For several weeks, Lucy had anticipated this eventuality with a mixture of eagerness and apprehension. And then suddenly, there it was - a duplicate of the first. Just a few words, cut from a magazine and accompanied by a photograph.

This time it was Maudie's husband, Ralph, who stepped up to the plate and took one for the team. There was no mistaking the verdant surrounds of the local water hole and no mistaking the imposing girth of the broad, white backside, breaking the water like a breaching whale, moonlight reflecting off its vast proportions. No one else in Daisy Plains could boast such an impressive derriere.

At the next lady's lunch, the whoops and hollers and squeals of delight issuing from the supper room, outdid even the first occasion in enthusiasm and brought the fascinated children running from the yard to see what was afoot. The day was warm, the wine cool, and before even the advent of afternoon tea the ladies had stripped to their scanties and run helter-skelter into the torrent of an unsuspecting neighbour's pivot irrigator, where they cavorted with the children until the shadows lengthened and the day grew chilly. Then, the ladies retreated to the sanctuary of Lucy's parlour to contemplate once again the author of these fascinating disclosures.

With the zeal of the newly converted, the ladies anticipated the advent of the next revelation with unrestrained excitement. Lucy's phone rang off the hook as the day of publication drew nearer. Have you heard yet? Has another arrived? Who do you think it will be this time? They enquired with unquenchable enthusiasm. Since the advent of the first disclosure, no one in Daisy Plains would dream of missing the Gazette. In fact, it had been mooted in some circles that the name of the newsletter be reinvented to Daisy's Exposé or some such other moniker more redolent of its invigorated content.

Lucy, however, was having misgivings. So far, the unsolicited content had pushed the boundaries of benign but what if the next revelation took a further step towards the dark side. She longed to know the author of the correspondence and to be reassured that no one would ultimately be hurt. Lucy was a kindly soul and not inclined to be the sponsor of vitriol. Was it possible they were being lulled by trivialities into accepting a life-destroying disclosure? Lucy vowed that should such an eventuality arise she would ensure it was never published. It was possible that the targets of these revelations had conspired amongst themselves to add spice to the lives of the local community. They had certainly taken the disclosures with unfailing good humour. But Lucy couldn't be sure.

The third exposé was wheelies at the drive-in theatre and then teens running amuck with a shopping trolley. Each time a new revelation was published, the debate as to the author became more heated. Lucy had researched the vexing question in depth, but her usual sources were mute. They either didn't know or wouldn't tell. And when, as a last-ditch effort, she approached the children, their response was guarded.

When the fifth exposé was shoplifting, it was time to take a stand. Somewhere deep inside, Lucy had known this day would come. True, it was only a magazine at the local newsagents, but she drew the line at crimes, no matter how minor.

Resolute, she marched out into the yard and marshalled the children. "I need something of interest for the paper," she began without preamble.

"How about we have a drawing competition and I put the winning picture in the paper." She lay out art supplies on her large outdoor table and wore her most winning smile.

"Didn't the mailman bring you something special today?" asked a cherub of a child, Eden, about ten years old with wide innocent eyes.

"Not this time," Lucy said, trying not to let her disappointment show.

"Look again." Elsie bounced on the spot, anticipation in her eyes.

Then the penny dropped, and Lucy's face flushed crimson. The teens in the group refused to meet her gaze. She remembered an old polaroid camera in one of the boxes of toys she'd cajoled from St Vincent de Paul's, and her open lament to the children about the paper's lack of content. She didn't know whether to chastise them or cuddle them. After all, they'd done it to please her.

"Oh dear," she said gently, looking around and feeling tears well in her eyes. "Let's all sit down and have a little talk."

The Green Coat

Tom Penrose

Sergeant Falstaff approached the murder scene with long purposeful strides. The hansom cab had dropped him at the corner, the cabbie reluctant to venture any further into this perilous part of Sydney town. Acrid smoke from early evening fires hung in the air forming a pungent mist. A constable of the Foot Patrol was standing guard over the fallen victim.

'Good evening constable, what have we here?'

'A Frank Daley, sir. He appears to have been struck several times on the back of the head with a heavy object.'

'When did this happen?'

'At five minutes past five, sir.'

'That's very exact.'

'There was a witness sir. Saw the whole thing. He's the man sitting outside of the hotel there with your Constable O'Grady.'

'Stay with the body and wait for the doctor, he'll be along shortly.'

Falstaff strode across the unevenly paved street where a man in working clothing was slumped in a chair outside the Royal Arms Hotel. He was hunched over with his head in his hands.

'Mr. Peter Bligh, sir,' said O'Grady.

'My name is Sergeant Falstaff; I believe you saw the incident.'

'That I did,' said Bligh, 'shocking it was, sir, shocking.'

'Constable, get Mr. Bligh a brandy.' Falstaff said, handing O'Grady a coin.

When the constable returned, and Bligh had taken a draught of the brandy, Falstaff continued.

'Tell me what you saw, Bligh. Take your time.'

'I was waiting outside the hotel for Frank, Frank Daly that is.'

'You were waiting outside, not inside?'

'Yes sir. You see I lost my work about a month ago and haven't been able to find employment. On Fridays, Frank collects his pay, meets me here and buys me a pint. I wait for him outside cos it doesn't seem right to stand inside without a drink.'

'I see, go on then.'

'Well, I seen Frank coming down the street, then, just as he passes that alley there, a man runs out behind him and hits him on the head with a club. Frank falls down and the man hits him again and runs back in the alley.'

'Could you describe this man?'

'No need, I'll tell you who it was. Jack Kelly.'

The Sergeant looks back up the gas-lit street to where Frank Daly was lying. He could see that the doctor had arrived.

'Are you sure? It's a fair distance and this smoke makes it difficult to see clearly.'

'I recognised his green check coat and his hat. I didn't catch his face, it all happened so quickly, but it was him. I know Jack, he drinks here, always wears the same coat. Last Friday he and Frank had a big quarrel, and Jack threatened him. It got so bad the landlord told Jack to get out.'

'Do you know what they argued about?'

'Well, I s'pose you'll find out soon enough. Jack thought Frank was, well, messing around with Jack's wife. Jack must have given her a bit of a thrashing because she up and left, went back to her mothers. Jack blamed Frank for breaking up his marriage.'

'Do you know where Jack lives?'

Giving information to a policeman was not normal for Bligh, but the event he had witnessed got the better of him and he reluctantly provided the address to the sergeant.

When the body had been removed and the doctor had gone Sergeant Falstaff and Constable O'Grady went to the address Bligh had given.

The Sergeant rapped on the door. After a few minutes, a voice from inside.

'Who is it?'

'Police, are you Jack Kelly?'

"What if I am?'

'We'd like a word.'

'What about?'

'I could yell through the door so all your neighbours will know your business, or you could let me in.'

Kelly cautiously opened the door. He was a stout man dressed in shirtsleeves. Falstaff and O'Grady showed their badges and Kelly reluctantly let them in. The house was extremely untidy, when they got to the kitchen the remains of an evening meal for one were on the table along with a half-bottle of rum.

Falstaff glanced around.

'Wife's gone to visit her mother,' Kelly said.

'Permanently, I heard,' said Falstaff.

'Nah, she'll be back. What's this about then?'

'Do you know a Frank Daly?'

'That bastard, wish I didn't.'

'He's dead,' said Falstaff bluntly. 'Someone bashed his head in.'

Kelly glanced from one policeman to the other.

'You think it was me, I've been at work all day and home all evening.'

'Do you own a green check coat?'

'Why, yes, I do.'

'May I see it please,' asked the Sergeant.

'It's not here,' said Kelly.

'Where is it?'

'Yesterday I caught the sleeve on an iron railing and ripped the button off, caused a hole. So, I took it to Marx, the tailor in Brent Street. He said I could pick it up on Monday afternoon. What's this about the coat?'

'The man who attacked Grady was wearing a green check coat. A witness said it was yours.'

'Couldn't be, my coat is with Marx. Wait a minute, somebody is trying to blame this on me.'

'Who would do that?' asked Falstaff.

'That's for you to find out,' Kelly's voice was rising, 'you're the police, that's your job.'

'I believe you had a row with Daly recently?'

'I didn't kill him. Somebody is trying to get me in trouble, no, worse, someone's trying to get me hanged.'

Kelly was becoming agitated and up on his feet, looking around the room at the doors and windows.

'Calm down, Mr Kelly.'

'Calm down.' he said rapidly, 'somebody didn't put on a hat and coat like yours and kill somebody did they?'

'We're not here to arrest you Mr. Kelly. Come down to the police station tomorrow morning and make a written statement to the constable on duty.'

'Can't read or write.'

'The constable will write the statement, bring someone who can read it to you, and you can make your mark. Now, where did you buy your coat?'

'Fowlers store on George Street.'

'Did anybody else know where you bought it.'

'Yeah, I told a few people I drink with. I got it at a fair price and said so.'

'Alright, that's enough for tonight, we'll look into it. Don't do anything silly, and don't think about going anywhere.'

They left the visibly shaken Kelly and hailed a cab to take them back to the station.

'What do you think Sergeant?' asked O'Grady as the cab rattled along the rough streets.

'I don't know. Tomorrow I'll go to Fowlers and see how many of those coats they sold. You can go and see Marx to make sure Kelly's coat is there and when it was dropped off.'

'Tomorrow's Saturday sir. Mr. Marx is, I believe, of the persuasion that doesn't do business on a Saturday.'

'I think you will find he has an apprentice who will be there. Old Marx will be wanting his man to finish the repairs by Monday.'

They met back at the police station mid-morning. The sergeant pulled a notebook from his pocket.

'Take this down Constable,' he said. 'I attended Fowlers store this morning and spoke to a Mr. Alistair Fowler, a junior member of the family. He stated that they had sold two of the said coats, one to a man answering Kelly's description and one to a man who may or may not have had an Irish accent. Mr. Fowler could not remember the man clearly enough to give a description, but the second sale was only last week. That's it, now don't write this down. I can see why people remembered the coat. It was very, shall I say, colourful. Now what about you at Marx the tailor?'

'You were right, there was a young man named Rossiter in the shop. He remembered the coat and showed it to me. I agree with your opinion of the garment, sir. He said he would repair it this morning and Mr. Marx would inspect it on Monday before Kelly picks it up.'

'Did he say when Kelly bought it in?'

'Yes, early on Friday afternoon.'

'So, it can't be the coat Bligh saw on Friday night.'

'If he did see the coat.'

'That thought had crossed my mind, but let's assume that he did see it. He was certainly shaken by what he'd seen. Now, you have all your notes from finding the body, talking to Kelly and Rossiter and mine from Fowlers. Can you put them all into one report for the Inspector? I'll go to see the landlord of the Royal Arms Hotel. He may be able to shed some further light on the matter.'

Falstaff's attempt to gain information from the landlord and patrons of the hotel was met with grunts and a collective loss of memory. He left wondering how they could be so unhelpful when one of their fellow drinkers had been brutally murdered.

Outside the hotel, an old man with rheumy eyes who had been drinking inside sidled up to him.

'Buy an old sailor a drink?' he rasped, holding out a shaking hand.

Falstaff was about to wave him away when the old man leaned closer.

'You must doubt Jack Kelly did it if yer still asking questions,' he whispered, 'yer might ask about Declan Kildare. He had a right barney with both Kelly and Daly couple of weeks back over a card game. Said they were both cheating him out of his money. Called them a lot of names and said they'd be sorry.'

Falstaff reached into his pocket and gave the old man a coin.

'Mighty kind,' said the old sailor in a louder voice, 'kind to an old man, an old sailor, thank you, sir.'

The old man went back inside. Another round of rum thought Falstaff.

When he arrived back at the police station Constable O'Grady seemed extremely excited.

'What is it, Constable?

'Well, sir, I was writing up my notes, like you asked, and I came across something interesting.'

He handed Falstaff his notes and pointed a line out. It took the sergeant a few seconds to realise the meaning of what was written.

'Well,' he said, 'that could explain a few things.'

He told the constable about his conversation outside the hotel and outlined to him how they would proceed.

Early that evening they visited Jack Kelly again.

'What do you want this time? Have you caught the bastard trying to get me hanged?'

'When I asked you if you knew who would want to blame the murder on you why didn't you mention Declan Kildare? Didn't he accuse both you and Daly of cheating him?'

'Declan reckons everyone cheats him, but he's just a terrible card player.' Kelly rubbed his chin. 'Now you mention it, that night he lost really heavily and was quite angry, more than usual, and I haven't seen him since.'

'Do you know where he lives?'

'No, no. I don't, somewhere near the wharves I think.'

'Never mind, I'm sure we can find out. You didn't come in and make a statement today.'

'No, I'll do it first thing Monday, I've got someone who will come with me to make sure you don't put anything I didn't say into it.'

'See you do. Good night.'

Five minutes past the hour of eleven and a figure carrying a calico bag emerged from the back gate and crept into the darkness of the alley behind the row of houses. It silently made its way towards the street. It had almost reached the corner when two men appeared in its path. The figure turned back but was startled to see another larger man approaching from the other end of the alley. Figuring there were better odds in taking on one than rather two the figure ran towards the single one with the aim of dashing around his larger rival. Unfortunately, the larger man was also quite agile and the attempt to sidestep it ended with a crashing tackle.

The furtive figure was trying to regain its breath when one of the men leant over it, took possession of the calico bag and said, 'Jack Kelly, I am arresting you for the murder of Frank Daly.'

'Good work,' said the Inspector later, 'has he confessed yet.'

'Not yet,' said Falstaff, 'but as I suspected there was the second green check coat in the bag with blood on the sleeve which I suspect belongs to Daly. I think he planned to plant it near the house of Declan Kildare once he knew we suspected him.'

'So, Kelly bought the second coat, caused a tear in the original one and gave it to the tailor to repair so to give himself an alibi and look as if he was being set up. Very clever. What gave him away?'

'You can thank Constable O'Grady. He pointed out that when he was protesting that somebody was setting him up, he said that anybody could put on a hat and coat like his and look like him.'

"Which means what?' asked the inspector.

'I never mentioned a hat.'

The Phantom

John Walker

I'd dabbled in short stories, but I wanted something more.

A murder mystery with a twist's what I was looking for.

I looked in vain for many months but then I got a call

"A phantom sighted in the grounds of old Fillongley Hall".

The papers told of spooky sightings down the lanes at night

And villagers from all around described their dread and fright.

The phantom glided by while making hardly any sound,

Save for a weird ticking which set off the local hounds.

Nothing ventured, nothing gained, I had to go and see

This scary place – Fillongley Hall – if they would talk to me.

To my surprise, my phone call then achieved that modest aim.

 "A novelist, are you? Please come in. Are you a famous name?"

I'm taken through the Entrance Hall, with inlaid-timber floor,

And massive marble pillars – are they Doric? I'm not sure!

And surely that's a Rembrandt up there hanging on the wall?

"I'm Lady Norton – Lizzie please –welcome to our Hall!"

I asked about the phantom, but she smilingly demurred.

"My husband knows the truth therein – in spite of what you've heard".

So, in due course, Lord Norton came and joined our little chat

"A great place for a murder then? I like the sound of that!

As setting for a murder, our home has got the lot.

It's up to you, dear novelist, to come up with the plot!"

So, as we walked around the grounds, I'm aching to find out

The story of the phantom, and how it came about!

 My patience was rewarded, and his Lordship gave a smile,

"I wondered if you'd heard of that – been hidden for a while!

 It all goes back to grandad's days when I was just a lad.

He died – some say was poisoned – left me everything he had".

"It could have happened any time – spent many years near death,

And he threatened that he'd haunt us with his very dying breath!"

But as he spoke, he turned a key to open the garage door.

"Voila!" he said, "Magnificent! This what you're looking for?"

I peered inside and there I saw the Phantom, there's no doubt!

A 1920s black Rolls Royce, the family runabout!

"Grandad bought it years ago. I just drive it 'round the park,

And sometimes down the foggy lanes 'round here after dark!"

He turned the key – the giant headlights gave a ghostly glow.

The motor was so quiet, if it's running, you wouldn't know.

But the clock – that quiet ticking – could that be what they heard?

My murder mystery theory began to seem a bit absurd!

Those reported apparitions, the lights, the ticking sounds

Were simply when Lord Norton drove his car around the grounds!

"So, what's left now of your well-thought-out phantom-murder plot?"

I nearly killed him there and then but thought I'd better not!

But a wicked thought - a story line, nobody knows I'm here!

Except for these two Nortons – and they could "disappear"!

Twisted

Louie Page

Surrounded by a heavy dampness, the eerie feeling was like a scene out of a Steven King novel. Her head spinning, her memory blurred from all those colourful drinks made the past and the present seem surreal. With her shoes dangling in her shivering fingers, she blearily looked down the main street with rows of darkened shop fronts. Desperate to get home, she decided to stick her thumb out to hitch a ride. She was staggering along on the side of the street, not knowing her next decision would be life altering. A car suddenly stopped; her hand grabbed the rear passenger's door handle. Instant relief overcame her. Clumsily, she climbed inside to the welcoming warmth, yet there was an odour which was unfamiliar and turned her stomach. The darkly bearded driver, his eyes narrow and his jaw clenched grumbled 'what are you doing?'

'Thanks for stopping mate, I need a lift home,' she slurred her answer.

'It's the third street ahead, my house is a couple of blocks down.'

Her words were almost unintelligible. The driver looked bewilderedly to his left at his partner and then turned back to the uninvited passenger in the rear.

'Give me your bag and keep your head down.'

Startled, she passed her bag over with shaking hands, her heart began to pound rapidly. She could almost hear its thumping beat. She wondered what to say.

'Keep it, there is money inside, it's yours' she pleaded to him.

The other front passenger looked over his shoulder.

'Shut up and put your seat belt on, we are going to take you for a little drive.'

She reached for the handle trying to get out. He heard her struggling.

'In this car, there is no way you can get out - and put your seatbelt on, I hate repeating myself.'

She was panicking but couldn't make out any features through her blurred eyes. A feeling of horror began to creep over her. She tried the door again, then the window. Reality slowly set in, she was trapped inside a speeding car, propelled backwards from the force of the acceleration.

They drove in silence. The bright light of a torch shone from the front seat. She could hear him rattling through her bag, opening her wallet, telling his partner the address of the place she calls home.

'There is more money at home' she admitted in a quivering voice. 'Turn here, this is my street.'

They kept driving straight ahead, into the darkness. Desperate and trembling, she looked behind and started to see the streetlights fading in the distance.

By this stage, her body was numbing with fear as reality set in. The car slowed down, then turned right. The road turned onto a bumpy track. Thick bushland surrounded them, and only dim light was visible in front of the car. At that point she started to pray to herself, eyes closed, head still tilted downwards.

'God, I have made a horrible mistake tonight, please help me,' she said aloud.

Suddenly, the driver slammed on the brakes, pushing her forwards against the seatbelt. Dust surrounded the car, it swirled through the headlights, dimming the lights even more.

The driver looked at her and spoke.

'You are praying to God, what took you so long?'

Shaken by the question, she struggled to understand what was about to happen.

'This is the biggest mistake of my life,' she said with her hands together in prayer. 'Please, please, I beg you, take me home.'

The driver looked over his shoulder, his eyes looking beyond her into the darkness. That was when she finally realized the car was now reversing. He changed gears and she could see they were heading back towards the main road. The town streetlights were visible in the distance again and slowly becoming larger, leaving the darkness behind. She sat there quietly thanking God in her mind.

They turned down a street she knew well and desperately longed for. The car came to a halt. She ripped the seatbelt off and began banging on the window, pushing hard on the door with her shoulder. The door was suddenly opened from the outside and she fell in the gutter. As quickly as she was down, she stood up, all drunkenness had evaporated. She scrambled backwards, looking at the man she had feared.

As he moved back into the car, he turned to her, and said, 'I hope you have learnt a lesson from this.'

She watched as the car door closed and the words on the doors became visible to her fogged brain.

The police car slowly drove away.

Who Forged the Land Title?

Susan Ash

The three men were huddled around the oil lantern on the table in the kitchen of the Fortunes of War. They thought she was asleep, just a teenage girl, exhausted after a long day sailing to Sydney Town, but Cat had woken to the sound of a thump on the table and raised voices. She kept her eyes closed and stayed curled around her younger sister on the couch. The fire flared in the grate and threw shadows into the lamplight. The sweet smell of burning tobacco from the pipes the men were smoking filled the darkened room and the smoke added to the haze. Cat watched them, ready to shut her half open eyes at their slightest turn in her direction. Jack's surprise was evident when he spoke,

'But this is Richard Willoughby's Certificate of Title for his land on Mangrove Creek!'

Jack had brought her down the coast in the little longboat, all the way from Wisemans at Lower Portland Head. At first he had resisted, thought it was too dangerous but she had prevailed. She had her Pa's grain to sell and she had brought her sister as company. Cat liked Jack, she felt safe with him. But she had not bargained on the seasickness during the journey and it had taken its toll. She was tired but she was not going to drowse off. Her interest was spiked by this conversation.

'Aye,' said a man she did not know.

'What is it doing here, Thomas?' asked Jack.

'It's a template, Jack,' said Duncan, Jack's sailing mate.

Duncan lived near Jack on Mangrove Creek. He had a reputation as a drinker and gambler and the effects of his lifestyle had given him a florid face and a belly.

'It's a template for what?' continued Jack.

'Well, for those who want to secure land but cannot afford the ten pounds. Those who have settled on the land and believe it to be theirs.'

'Like you, Duncan. Someone who gambles away his money. What are you suggesting? Surely not forging this document.' Jack's voice rose.

'Quiet, man!'

Thomas turned and looked across at the sleeping pair on the couch. Cat kept her eyes firmly shut. The three men lowered their voices and she could no longer hear Jack's next response. Soon they stood and moved out into the gloomy depths of the Fortunes of War. All she heard as they left were Jack's final words,

'I will not be drawn into this.'

Cat did not fall asleep for a long time after they left. She knew forgery was a crime in the colony. Her Pa had told her people hung for the crime. Her gut clenched. Could Jack hang if he was caught? She did not want anything to happen to Jack, certainly not for him to hang.

She wanted to ask Jack more about land titles on their return journey but she was wary of Duncan sitting in the bow of the longboat, so said nothing. It was only when they were tying the boat up at the wharf that Duncan said,

'That was quite a night's work. I'm looking forward to getting back to my own land on Mangrove.'

What could this mean? Had Jack made the forged copy?

'You know I refuse to do anything illegal,' was Jack's reply. Cat relaxed.

'But you have the best hand in the colony,' Duncan laughed.

Cat watched Jack set his shoulders in anger and stride off without a word. There were crowds around the wharf and her Pa was waiting.

'Here's the money from the sale of the grain.' Cat was flushed with pleasure at her success.

'Come away, Cat,' her Pa's anxious tone alarmed her. 'I should'na have sent you with these two.'

'Why not, Pa? It was fine.'

'Jack has been called to the Magistrate's court in Windsor. A Certificate of Title has been forged.'

Cat's heart sank. She could not believe Jack would commit a crime. She realised then she was just a little bit in love with Jack. He had been gentle with her. Not in any inappropriate way, just concerned about her sickness on the voyage. And he had helped her sell her grain. He seemed to admire her feistiness. And she was just a little annoyed that her Pa did not think her capable of judging the trustworthiness of these men.

She watched in horror as the Magistrate put irons on Jack's wrists and led him away to the watchhouse. She had no thoughts of danger when put on her stout leather boots and set out over the ridge to Mangrove Creek where she knew Duncan would be returning. She wanted to hear from him what had happened in Sydney. He was pulling into the jetty, as she came down the slope.

'Well, Miss Cat, what can I do for you? Perhaps a cup of tea?' he said.

'That would be good. I've a thirst on me.'

They settled around the fire on the wooden stumps he used for seats.

'That was quite a trip to Sydney,' Duncan said after a while, his red face glowing a little in the fire's reflection.

Cat was slightly repulsed by him but she knew he responded well to flattery and she wanted more information.

'Yes,' she paused, thinking carefully. 'If I were to marry and settle around here, what would a husband need to show me. You know, so I could be sure he owned the land.'

'Well,' Duncan's interest was spiked. 'Thinking of marriage, Miss Cat?' He took a gulp of tea. 'The Certificate of Title which would have his name on it, the date he purchased it and the Gov'nor's signature.'

'Would you be able to show me your title?' she said innocently.

'Well, now you ask, I just have such a thing.' He pulled the document out of his pocket and spread it on the makeshift table.

'Can you trace out the words for me? I still have trouble with my letters.'

'There's my name – Duncan Stewart' he pointed to the script, 'and the date.'

She recognised the numbers. It said 8th May but she knew they were only in the month of April and the year was the one just past. 'Can you read the numbers for the year?'

'Oh,' said Duncan, 'it's this year, 1834.' He looked at her with increasing attention. He held no suspicion that she knew the date was incorrect and that the title might be false.

'So, you own this land?'

'Why yes, it was all sorted out while we were in Sydney. That Thomas, he helped me a great deal.' He looked admiringly at Cat. 'And would you be interested in living here on this land?' He paused, 'with me?'

'I might,' she said, suppressing the revulsion rising in her gut, 'but tell me a bit more about this Thomas.'

'Oh, he was transported with Jack. They were caught forging notes in London. Thomas has worked hard here but he's not past using the skills from his old crime. He has a way of giving friends a helping hand when they need it. Or if he needs a bit of extra cash.' Duncan was warming to his subject, gloating a little. 'If Thomas loses too much at cards or his friends do, he sometimes uses his skills to make some new notes, extra cash. Forged ones.'

'And land titles?' Cat wondered how far she could go with this. 'This was Mr Willoughby's land before, wasn't it?'

'Aye, that it was.' Duncan looked at her carefully. She smiled at him, egging him on.

'What happened to Mr Willoughby's Certificate?'

'Oh, we got up to a bit of trickery at the Fortunes of War. Not Jack. Jack didn't want anything to do with it. We snitched Willoughby's Certificate when he was drunk, Thomas and I. Thought we'd make a copy. But in the end, it was not necessary. He wanted to sell. He had lost all his money gambling ... and I got a bargain! This is my land now.' He sat back and rubbed his ample stomach.

Cat knew this to be a lie. The dates were wrong. 'Why is the date wrong, then?'

Duncan looked at her sharply. 'Not so innocent after all, are you Missy Cat?' He stood up and went to grab hold of her, a malevolence darkening his face. 'So, you think you can trap me, do you?' His laugh was full of derision. 'Do you think the Magistrate will believe a young slip of girl, like you?'

The anger bloomed in Cat's chest. 'What kind of a friend are you? Letting Jack take the blame for a forged document?'

'Is it a forgery though? It would be your word against mine, Miss Smarty Pants.'

He went to grab her again. She snatched up the Land Title, turned and fled up the hill, knowing her young legs could outrun Duncan. She had the evidence now but what

109

was she going to do with it and who indeed would believe her?

You Won't Get Away With It

Janice McLachlan

Startled awake, Tristan shot out of bed. The distinctive odour of smouldering electricals wafted through her door, followed by the sound of fireworks. Heart thumping, she scurried down the stairs, tripping over her feet in her haste. Glass baubles lay shattered around her treasured Christmas Tree; tinsel smouldered and flamed; the faces on her heirloom nutcrackers drooped and sagged like toy soldiers with a bad case of palsy.

Tristan stifled a shriek.

"That's what he wants, a reaction from you," the counsellor had cautioned.

Tristan gazed up at the blackened branches and melted ornaments to the apex of the tree, unsurprised to see her precious fairy was gone.

There was no use accusing Andy. He would deny it. But she knew it was him. Just as she knew, her golden-haired child would have an ironclad alibi and offer some jibber-jabber about his imaginary friend, Charlie.

The counsellor had tried to explain, "You love Christmas and Andy is jealous."

If Tristan had believed that were true, it would have been some consolation, but she didn't. Christmas brought out the worst in Andy. He'd been adopted as a newborn, but Tristan no longer believed nurture trumped nature.

"He's just a child needing attention," said the Counsellor, making Tristan feel as if the fault lay with her. "Perhaps you should forget Christmas for a year or two."

But Andy had crossed a line when he'd stolen Tristan's Christmas fairy and Tristan hardened her heart.

Next time, she prepared in secret. Pretending there would be no Christmas with such poise she had Andy convinced. He gasped when he saw it. A hurriedly assembled tree without the intoxicating flashing lights or glittering baubles of previous years. Instead, there was only tinsel. Andy hated tinsel. Fluffy swirls, in silvery swathes, wound up the tree's pristine branches, and at the top, another Christmas fairy.

"You won't get away with it," Andy fumed.

"Where are the lights?" he demanded, hands on skinny hips, lips pouting, when Tristan came through the door.

"I'm sorry, darling," she said, "but I thought after last time, well, you know."

"That wasn't my fault. It was Charlie." Andy cursed.

"You know the Counsellor said we're not to blame Charlie." Tristan replied.

"No good without lights." Andy scowled and stomped his feet. When scowling didn't work, he raged and threw himself on the floor. "I want lights. I want lights."

But Tristan stood firm.

"What do you think, Charlie?" Andy hissed, later that night. "I reckon that bloody fairy is just asking to be bashed, beaten, and burnt. Don't you?"

"Yes, yes, you're right. It's all that miserable counsellor lady's fault." Andy brightened. "Miss Jayne, Miss Pain! She doesn't like that. Does she? No sense of humour."

"The hide of her telling Mum you're not real."

"Yes, I was offended too."

"Oooh, good idea. You are the clever one." Andy snickered. "I'll get the matches and we'll pay that pain a visit. We'll show her who's real."

You Won't Get Away with It

Kerry Buchanan

'Come on Willis. You won't get away with it. Your old mate Jaxon is next door singing his little heart out. If you don't want to take the wrap for the whole sorry mess, it's time you started talking too.'

Willis stayed silent.

Detective Maddison made a face as if she'd just sucked a lemon. She looked at Willis and shook her head. Then she turned to the young officer beside her.

'So, what was it that Jaxon said, Sergeant Jones? Something about him not knowing anything about a robbery?'

'Yes M'am. He said his friend Willis called to ask if he'd drive his truck and help to collect a few things.'

Detective Maddison turned back to Willis. 'Jaxon said he got the surprise of his life when you came running out of the building wearing a balaclava and carrying a bag of cash.'

'Jaxon doesn't have a record either, M'am.' said the Sergeant. 'Not even a parking ticket.'

Willis sat back in his chair. 'Jax wouldn't say nothing. You're not foolin' me. Like I said, I was at me girls' place. Bethany. Go and ask her.'

Detective Maddison's voice took on a whiny tone. 'Go and ask her? Well, we did. And of course, she said you were there. For a bit. She also said she saw Jaxon that same evening. Still, I guess that was after you left.'

'Or before he got there, M'am,' said the Seargent.

'Yeah. I guess that'd work,' smiled the detective.

'What are you talking about?' Willis's brow furrowed.

'Oh, you didn't know? Turns out Bethany and Jaxon have a little secret. We found plane tickets to Ibiza and all. I think she's planning on leaving next week.'

'Not much of a girlfriend, M'am,' said the sergeant.

'Not much of a friend either, hey Willis?' said the detective.

Willis sat stiff in the metal chair. Bethany had only told him last night that she was going to Ibiza. She was supposed to be going with her sister. And then when he'd told her about the robbery, she asked him not to come around again.

'I don't need social services on my back, Willis,' she'd said. Willis started to sweat. Oh, Jaxon had told the truth all right. Only thing was, Willis had been the one surprised. Jaxon had tricked him into driving. Now the bastard was trying to stitch him up. And steal his girl too.

'Okay, I'll tell you what really happened. That bloody Jaxon's not going to get away with it.'

Sergeant Jones and Detective Maddison watched as the guards led Willis and Jaxon past each other, on their way down to the holding cells.

'Ya' bloody idiot,' Jaxon cried. Why'd ya' go and talk ya' weasel? They had nothin!'

'Why'd ya' go and steal my girl? Ya' slimy bastard.

'What are ya' talkin' about? You fool!' called Jaxon.

Detective Maddison looked at Sergeant Jones. 'And that's a wrap,' she said smiling.

'Nice job, M'am,' replied Jones.

'Coffee?' he asked.

You Won't Get Away With It

Rachel Rose

Marcia's third day of collecting for the heart foundation took a nasty turn. Lots of people donated, and she enjoyed the friendly chats, but at the next house everything changed. Admiring some carved wooden statues beneath a window, she pulled out her phone to snap them. A rough voice, and even rougher shove sent her flying across the verandah and through the open door, where the voice addressed two other people.

"I spotted this bird snoopin' around outside, must've heard our plans. We'll have to keep her quiet and out of the way 'til after the pick-up."

Marcia reacted.

"Hey! I wasn't prowling, I came to ask for a donation. Mr George donates every year, where is he?" The rough stranger ignored her. Then she was bound, gagged and manhandled into a semi-dark shed, the door was slammed shut and locked. Shocked and afraid, then angry, Marcia rolled onto her side, then onto her knees. With her feet crossed and bound together, she couldn't stand, and things looked bad.

'Must get my hands free,' she thought, 'find something sharp.'

She pulled herself along on her bottom, searching for tools.

Somewhat later, she had removed the gag, cut her bonds, and her hands, on the teeth of a steel garden rake. Her hands were free but as her bleeding fingers fumbled with her ankle bonds the door flew open. She lay back, hiding her hands behind her back, but not quick enough.

The ruffian stormed at her. "Getting clever, are we? You won't get away with it." He shouted to the other men to 'hurry with the packages and bring me the Indian'. Struggling fruitlessly, Marcia was encased in the back half of a hollow statue, then the front half clipped into position. She stood on tip toe to reach the open mouth of the tall warrior, but fear made her breathing hard to control.

'I must stay calm, wish the brute hadn't stolen my phone,' she thought.

Packed into a huge van, upright, she tried to tilt the statue and move it toward the back door, but the effort made her breathless. What seemed hours later, the van stopped. She felt fresher air, smelled food cooking and the sounds of an outdoor market. As statues were removed, she rocked back and forth until the statue toppled, then rolled out the open door. The heavy landing took its toll, but when she heard the van driver say, "Sorry mate, that one's supposed to stay, other plans for it", she became desperate. Through the statue mouth, she called, "No! Help me, let me out! Help, please help!"

Security and police swooped, and Marcia was free.

Police, market personnel and Mr George all said she was brave, and had solved the mystery of how some dealers had smuggled their drugs interstate. Mr George had been threatened and forced to make hollow statues for them.

Marcia's crush on Mr George was kept secret, though.

About Port Writers

Port Writers Inc is an incorporated not-for-profit community group which aspires to support and help writers and authors in all genres.

Formed in 2016 as an inclusive writing group for the Port Macquarie, Hastings and Camden areas we are proud to have hobby writers, amateur writers, serious writers and published authors amongst our membership. Interests range from fiction to memoir to poetry, from Crime to Romance to Children's, and everything in between. Port Writers focus is on providing support, encouragement and skills development to help members enjoy and explore their writing journey.

Every fourth Saturday of the month from January to October we get together to learn, discuss, write and support each other. Guest presenters are invited from time to time to lead talks or workshops to further develop our writing knowledge. And we grab the chance for an informal coffee catch up every month, too.

Our National Open Writing Competition includes an extra Prize for local authors to further inspire writers in the Port Macquarie Hastings area. Check our website for details.

www.portwiters.com.au

or connect with us at www.facebook.com/portwriters/

www.ingramcontent.com/pod-product-compliance
Lightning Source LLC
Chambersburg PA
CBHW051232210726
48290CB00003B/923